MARNIE'S QUEST

In every generation dawns a most auspicious day,
The day when four elevens meet and Sleepers have their say,
The day to which the fickle sands of time and tide have run,
The day when fate and prophecy reveal the Chosen One.

BBC CHILDREN'S BOOKS

Published by the Penguin Group
Penguin Books Ltd, 80 Strand, London WC2R 0RL, England
Penguin Group (USA) Inc., 375 Hudson Street, New York, New York 10014, USA
Penguin Group (Australia) Ltd, 250 Camberwell Road, Camberwell, Victoria, 3124, Australia
(a division of Pearson Australia Group Pty Ltd)
Canada, India, New Zealand, South Africa

Published by BBC Children's Books, 2005

10 9 8 7 6 5 4 3 2 1

ISBN 1 405 90104 7

Printed in the United Kingdom

MARNIE'S QUEST

Adapted by Kay Woodward from a story
created by CBBC Scotland and Brian Ward

CHAPTER ONE

The Magic Is Awakened

Marnie McBride was eleven years old. That's to say, at precisely eleven minutes past eleven that morning – the eleventh day of the eleventh month – she would be eleven years old. A cause for celebration, you'd think. But not for Marnie. Her mother had died barely two months earlier – and Marnie had not yet shed a tear.

"Go on, blow them out and make a wish," said Dad.

Marnie looked unhappily at the flickering candles poking out of her birthday cake. Dad was trying his hardest to make this the perfect day, but she couldn't ignore the fact that there was one vital ingredient missing. With a heavy heart, Marnie made her wish – a wish that she knew could never come true. She wished that her mother would come back. One melancholy breath later and the tiny flames were extinguished.

1

"Are you going to open your presents?" asked Dad gently.

Marnie forced a smile and reached for a parcel.

Later that morning, Dad had tried everything he could think of to lift Marnie's spirits. Unfortunately, not all of his ideas were as stunning as her cake.

"Did you enjoy that?" he asked, as they left the University Library. He'd given Marnie the grand tour, introduced her to his new colleagues and shown her where he'd be working.

Marnie smiled, pushing blonde hair out of her eyes. "Yeah, it was cool," she said kindly. Her dad was trying hard to be cool too, but a birthday cake, a heap of presents and a million shelves of books weren't going to cheer her up. No, Marnie needed something more. The problem was – and it was quite a big problem – she just didn't know what.

"Mind if I take a look, Marnie?" said Dad, inter-rupting her thoughts.

Somehow, they'd wandered into a dingy backstreet that Marnie didn't recognise. That wasn't surprising – it was only a couple of weeks since they'd left the States and come to live in Edinburgh. But the street was weird, there was no doubt about it – crumbling brickwork, uneven cobbles, gloomy arches that led to goodness knows where. And empty too, apart from one peculiar old shop – its windows full of dusty books and with a jumble of junk on the pavement outside. The faded sign said: 'Lost and Found'.

Dad grinned. "You never know, I might find a first edition."

Marnie sighed. It was OK for Dad – librarians liked these sorts of places. She tried to summon up enthusiasm, but the truth was, she didn't really care where they went. After the briefest of pauses, she followed him up the steps.

If the shop had seemed slightly odd from the outside, it was positively bizarre inside: shelves groaning with cracked ornaments; walls plastered with badly drawn pictures. It was a wonder anyone ever bought anything at all.

A curious sound rang through the shop and Marnie looked up to see the shop owner standing behind piles of crumbly this and faded that. Had he been there all along? Marnie didn't think so, but she couldn't be sure and her skin prickled uncomfortably.

The man was even stranger than his shop. His clothes were so old-fashioned that they would have been more at home in a museum. His hair was silver and his face creased and worn with age. His eyes were curiously unsettling – sharp, piercing and very dark. Marnie couldn't decide whether they looked kind or cruel.

"A book lover like myself," he said, his voice a low growl, "and just in time!" He hurried to close the door behind them. "For you, sir, a rare first edition, hmm?"

"Well, yes…" said Dad, as the shop owner steered him towards an untidy pile of books.

"And for you, young lady…" the shop owner muttered urgently, "…whatever takes your fancy."

Marnie glanced around, the ticking of the shop's antique clock growing louder and louder until it echoed inside her mind. Shadows began to gather in the corners of the shop and the atmosphere became charged with energy. It suddenly seemed to Marnie as though something amazing – or perhaps terrifying – was about to happen.

Then she saw it – there among the shabby books and chipped ornaments was a dog-eared and dusty old shoebox.

The shop owner leaned closer to Marnie. "Go on," he murmured menacingly. "They won't bite."

Marnie flinched. This guy was seriously weird. But, as if tugged by an invisible thread, she walked slowly towards the shoebox and slowly, nervously, lifted the lid. Inside were four figures – dusty, ancient and beautifully carved.

There was a thin, tarnished snake, fashioned not from a single piece of metal, but many tiny, patterned links. Its head was a masterpiece of metalwork – sleek and beautiful, yet dangerous-looking. There was even a tiny, forked tongue between its sharp fangs.

Marnie looked closely at the brown bear and realised that it was made of stone, each ripple of fur intricately crafted. Round its neck, it wore a band of dull colour.

She couldn't say why, but Marnie thought it looked the friendliest of the bunch.

The wooden wolf was perfectly carved, from the tips of its alert ears to the end of its pointed tail. Its coat was painted blue and gold, although this was masked by countless years of grime. At first glance, the wolf's feet looked black, but then Marnie saw that they were charred, as if by flames.

Finally, there was a short, squat eagle, made from dullish grey and yellow metals and clad in an armoured breastplate and helmet. His wings were totally mismatched: one was wide and sweeping, with perfect, curved feathers, while the other was clunky and unwieldy, made from pieces of scrap metal. Marnie guessed that it had been repaired at some time. But what struck her most was the eagle's proud expression – it was *so* lifelike. She carefully lifted it from the shoebox and stared closely. This – like all the others – looked much too special to be a toy.

Bong…! The clock chimed into the silence and Marnie jumped. Eleven times it chimed, the sounds bouncing eerily around the dark, gloomy old place. She glanced back at the eagle and got an even bigger shock.

The eagle blinked.

And the shop owner moved closer, beginning to chant strange words in a low, mesmerising whisper…

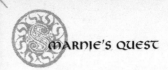

"In every generation dawns a most auspicious day,
The day when four elevens meet and Sleepers have their say,
The day to which the fickle sands of time and tide have run,
The day when fate and prophecy reveal the Chosen One."

OK, now Marnie was totally spooked. Four elevens? The Chosen One? She dropped the eagle back into the shoebox as if she'd been stung.

"Hasn't struck for eleven centuries," hissed the man. "How peculiar."

Dad came over, looking more than a little nervous. "Let's go home," he said to Marnie.

"Home," said the shop owner softly, almost threateningly. "Yes, you must take them home."

Dad peered into the shoebox. "What are those?" he asked.

Marnie could feel the shop owner's eyes burning into her. "Just a bunch of stupid toys," she said quickly.

The shop owner smiled knowingly. Then, as if he'd remembered a pressing engagement, he ushered his customers out of the gloom and into bright daylight, slamming and locking the door behind them.

"How much are they?" asked Dad, frowning at the carved animals.

"Nothing!" said the shop owner. "*Nada! Rien!* Consider them a gift, a mere trifle, my bibliophilic friend. After all, it is the young lady's birthday." Abruptly, he rushed away and was swallowed by the darkness of a nearby alley.

Dad frowned. "How did he know it was your birthday?" he said.

Marnie didn't know. She certainly hadn't told him.

Long after the sun had set on Marnie's eleventh birthday, she gazed blankly at the shoebox creatures. She'd hoped the eagle's blink had signalled the beginning of something that might help to take her mind off the pain of losing Mom, or at least help her to feel at home in this weird country. But all her hopes had added up to big, fat zero.

There was a knock at her bedroom door.

"Hey, birthday girl," said Dad. "I guess that's it for another year."

Marnie looked at the photo of her mother and swallowed. Sometimes, it was just so hard – the hardest thing she'd ever had to bear. "I miss Mom!" she burst out.

"I know. So do I, sweetheart," Dad said, hugging his daughter tightly. Then he lifted the shoebox lid. "Can I take a look at your wee friends?"

Marnie nodded glumly.

Dad picked up the wolf. "Wouldn't want to meet him on a dark night. Arrghhh!" he said. Then he lifted out the bear. "He's got a funny face. Your mum would've liked this one, wouldn't she?"

At this, Marnie's unhappiness threatened to rush to the surface once more. But, for the millionth time, she managed to hold her feelings inside.

Dad put the animals back in their shoebox and closed the lid. "Time for bed," he said. "Come on, in you get."

Marnie snuggled under the covers, relieved beyond words that her birthday was over. Now she could get back to normal – whatever that was.

"Sleep well," said Dad.

All was dark. All was still. All was quiet. Well, nearly all was quiet.

"Is the child asleep?" whispered a pompous voice from inside the shoebox.

"I don't know, Edwin," whispered another voice.

"Well, perhaps you'd oblige me by taking a look," replied the first voice.

"When did you ssstart giving the ordersss?" yet another voice hissed.

"When you're prepared to shoulder the burden of responsibility, Ailsa," whispered the first voice, "*you* can give the orders."

There was a cross hiss and then more whispered argument inside the shoebox before the lid slowly lifted. A pair of eyes blinked in the darkness. Then, one by one, four curious heads appeared over the side of the box. The eagle, the snake, the bear and the wolf were no longer models – they were alive…

Crack! A great flash of lightning illuminated the room and Marnie's computer exploded into life. The four animals cowered in terror as a golden mask blazed on the monitor and began to speak in a deep, menacing voice:

"*This is Michael Scot from whom you stole and who holds you in enchantment until your debt to me is repaid. Now get back into the chamber to which you are confined and do not dare leave until your new Master calls!*"

The shoebox lid banged shut, Marnie turned over in her sleep and the golden mask slowly faded from the screen – until it was gone.

the chosen one speaks

arnie awoke with a start to find sunlight flooding her bedroom. In the distance, a great bell chimed as she struggled to remember the weird dreams that had tormented her sleep. It was no use – they'd vanished with the night. But she couldn't rid herself of the nagging feeling that they had something to do with the four toys she had been given. She looked curiously at the shoebox. Dreams or no dreams, Marnie knew exactly what she was going to do with the toys inside.

One hour and a lot of scrubbing later, Marnie announced proudly, "If you *are* just toys, at least you're cleaned up now." She put the bear – his chiselled brown fur gleaming – on to the kitchen table, beside his three sparkling companions. Then she slurped a mouthful of cereal, keeping her eyes fixed firmly on the creatures.

"Abracadabra!" Marnie said jokingly, waving her

spoon like a wand. "Shazzam! Boom-calla-boom!" And again, "Awake! Awake, slumbering creatures... awake! For I am your *master*!"

At once, the creatures came to life.

Marnie gasped, ducked and crouched under the table, her eyes wide. She waited...and then she decided to take another look, peeping cautiously over the edge of the table. The trembling creatures stared back at Marnie.

Impatiently, and with a flick of her patterned tail, the green-eyed snake pushed the eagle forward. He held a clanking, metal wing in front of him and took a graceful bow. Then he spoke. "What do you command, oh Master?"

"Hey, I'm asking the questions, right?" said Marnie. This was just too weird. But, weird or not, she wasn't about to be bossed around by anyone, least of all a boxful of talking toys. "So, who are you?" she demanded.

The eagle puffed out his chest, rattling his armour importantly. "With due deference and respect, Master," he said haughtily, "we might well ask *you* the same question."

"Are you the Chosen One?" growled the blue and gold wolf, ignoring the angry looks that the others were sending in his direction.

"What's the Chosen One?" asked Marnie.

The eagle smiled knowledgeably. "That's for us to know and you to worry about—"

Enough was enough. Grasping a wing between her

11

finger and thumb, Marnie swung the bird into the air and dangled him there. "You're a cheeky little guy, whoever you are," she said.

"Oh, unhand me! Desist!" shouted the bird dramatically. "Put me down!"

"Not until you tell me your names," said Marnie.

"Don't tell her, Edwin!" boomed the bear.

The snake sighed heavily and shook her head.

"Oh, so you're Eddie the eagle, huh?" Marnie grinned at the eagle. This was going well – one name down, three to go. She turned her attention to the bear. "And you are…?"

"Bruno, your…your…uh, your Mastership," he mumbled.

"And you…?" Marnie placed a finger on the snake's tail to stop her slithering away.

"Ailsa," the creature hissed crossly. "As if it'sss any of *your* businesss!"

The wolf revealed his name without even being asked. "I am Wolfgang," he whispered. "But I'm not really one of *them*."

"OK, so I know, like, *who* you are," said Marnie, "but I don't know *what* you are."

"Well," said Eddie, slowly and clearly, "I am an eagle, he is a bear–"

"Don't be smart, Eddie," snapped Marnie. Boy, this eagle could be tiresome. "If I woke you up, I'll bet I can send you back to sleep."

Instantly, the creatures froze.

"No, stop!" said Marnie desperately. This wasn't what she wanted at all. "Awake! Awake, slumbering creatures. Awake, I command you!"

Nothing happened.

"Look, I'm sorry, OK?" Marnie pleaded. "I didn't mean to hurt your feelings."

But they remained silent and still.

After a moment, Marnie put the creatures back into the shoebox. Her mind was whirling. There was no way she'd imagined it. She *knew* that she'd just seen them come to life. But who would believe her? No one.

Except perhaps for the silver-haired old man at the junk shop…

Later that day, Marnie retraced her steps to the dingy backstreet, over the uneven cobbles and past the gloomy arches. But she found that the junk shop was boarded up. The useless junk, the dusty books and the cracked ornaments had all vanished. And so had the owner.

That evening, a small white aeroplane touched down at Edinburgh Airport. Its only passenger was tall, slim and immaculately dressed in a suit so white it seemed to glow. His hair was cropped close to his head and he wore a neat goatee beard. The man stepped gracefully from the aircraft and rode the short distance to the waiting car in an airport buggy.

"Señor Toledo?" asked McTaggart the chauffeur

eagerly. He received no reply. "Er…Balmoral Hotel, is it, sir?" he added.

Toledo looked disdainfully down his long, elegant nose at the short, scruffy chauffeur. "First, I'd like to go somewhere else," he drawled in an English accent.

"Very good, sir. Very good…yes, yes," stammered the chauffeur, stumbling under the unexpected weight of Toledo's luggage – a sturdy case made of dark wood and decorated with gold hinges and a clasp. Its lid was set with four metal domes.

"Be very, very careful," warned Toledo. "Don't shake them."

Them? McTaggart looked suspiciously at the case as the visitor climbed inside the sleek, white car and closed the door. He gently shook it. Strange, groaning sounds came from within.

Immediately, the window slid down to reveal Toledo's sneering face. "And I'll thank you to address me in a manner that more befits someone of my station, Mr McTaggart," the man snapped, before the window hid him from view once more.

"Beelzebub," McTaggart muttered to himself.

The Devil.

Its engine purring like a particularly satisfied cat, the white car glided over the cobbles, coming to a stop outside the deserted junk shop. McTaggart leapt to attention and rushed to open the car door for Toledo.

Boom! Boom! Boom!

McTaggart spun round.

Somehow, Toledo was already at the boarded-up door, pounding his fist against it. "*Abre! Soy Juan Roberto Montoya de Toledo!*" His voice echoed in the gloom.

"I don't think anybody's at home, your…your Magnificentness," said McTaggart nervously.

"*Abre! Les ordeño!*" Toledo ordered. The locked, bolted and boarded door was no match for him – it fell with a resounding clang into the empty shop, sending clouds of dust billowing into the air. Like an animal searching for its prey, Toledo walked forward. He sniffed deeply, then closed his eyes, raising his hands high. A beautiful ring glinted on one long, slender finger.

With a start, his eyes snapped open and a smile spread slowly across Toledo's face. "*Les hé encontrado!*" he announced triumphantly. "I have found you!"

At that exact moment, Marnie's creatures awoke, four sets of frightened eyes blinking in the darkness of the shoebox.

"He's found us!" squeaked Edwin.

"*He's* found us?" said Bruno, sounding confused.

"No, not *him*, ssstupid!" Ailsa whispered.

"Toledo – the Shapeshifter!" Wolfgang growled impatiently.

"We must flee!" cried Edwin, flapping his wings in panic. "Scram, vamoose, skedaddle! We have to get out of here!"

Marnie looked up from her desk and frowned at

15

the shoebox. Could she hear whispering? She was just about to investigate when Dad walked in.

"Have you finished?" he asked.

Marnie shook her head glumly. She hadn't even started her new school and *already* she had homework.

"It's not punishment," said Dad gently. "It's supposed to help you. The school needs to know what stage you're at so they can fit you in with the new curriculum." He patted her shoulder. "It's a big day tomorrow. And I know it's new and unfamiliar, but—" He was interrupted by the phone's insistent ringing.

On the other side of Edinburgh, inside the great clock tower of the Balmoral Hotel, Toledo was relaxing on a long, white sofa. Clad in a beautiful dressing gown, embroidered slippers and turban – all white – he stretched lazily and spoke into his mobile phone. "Am I addressing Mr McBride?"

"Yes…" said Marnie's dad slowly.

"Forgive the intrusion. You see, I'm a collector of antiques. And you purchased, yesterday, some figurines in which I have an *especial* interest." Toledo's voice was persuasive, but his eyes were full of menace. "Sir, I'd be prepared to pay handsomely for those little figures – if they are the ones I seek."

"How did you get my number?" asked Mr McBride.

"Let's just say we collectors have our tricks of the trade," replied Toledo smoothly. Then his voice changed. "I'm a busy man, Mr McBride. Can we do business or not?"

But Mr McBride had had enough. "Look, I don't know you and I don't know where you got my number," he said crossly, "and I don't much like the tone of your voice. The figurines were a birthday present and they're not for sale, all right?" He hung up.

Thoughtfully, he wandered back to Marnie's room. "Mind if I take a wee look at your friends in the shoebox?" he asked.

Marnie shrugged. "Sure," she said. But inside she felt a little knot of fear that her creatures would choose this moment to move or speak again. Suddenly, she knew that this was a secret she wanted to keep to herself.

Dad lifted the shoebox lid and they both peered inside. Marnie couldn't believe her eyes – the box was totally empty. "They were there a minute ago, I promise," she said.

Dad laughed. "So they just took the lid off and walked off by themselves, did they?"

Marnie's eyes darted suspiciously round her bedroom. She'd only known them for a, day, but she wouldn't be surprised if this was *exactly* what the shoebox animals had done.

"I don't think this is such a good idea," grumbled Wolfgang. He was sitting at the very top of a very long banister that spiralled down the stairs and out of sight.

"Rubbish," said Edwin, perched behind him.

"Escaping from the Chosen One's abode was the difficult part. I thought we'd never get through that great metal flap in the door. All we've got to do now is get out of the building – and then we're free!"

From the expressions on their faces, it was clear that his three accomplices weren't convinced of the wisdom of Edwin's plan, but–

"Ready?" said Edwin. "One…two…three…um… *go*!"

They were off! Huddled together like a bobsleigh team, they slid down the polished banister. Down, down, down they went, round and round, going faster and faster, until – *thwack*! They crashed straight into the post at the end of the banister and came to a dead stop. *Thud, thud, thud, thud* – they fell one by one on to the carpet below.

Two pink slippers arrived beside them. "Going somewhere?" asked Marnie, grinning with relief. Then she gathered the creatures into her arms and started back up the stairs.

It was lucky for the Shoebox Zoo that Marnie had foiled their escape because outside, there was evil in the air. A gleaming white car sped down the street, heading for the towering mansion block where Marnie lived. But someone was waiting for it to arrive. To Marnie and her dad, he had appeared as a junk shop owner. Others knew him to be a great wizard. As the car drew closer, he stepped from the pavement into its path.

McTaggart slammed on the brakes and screeched to a halt, brakes squealing, tyres smoking. Toledo stared disdainfully from the back seat. In a blinding flash of light, he vanished, only to materialise outside the car, leaning casually against the roof. "Ah, the great Michael Scot…" he drawled. "A little overdressed for the occasion, huh?"

The great wizard stood tall, his billowing robes edged with shimmering Celtic runes, an ebony and silver staff clasped in his hand. "Your lifetime is over," said Michael Scot calmly. "Your dark days are numbered."

"In elevens, I presume…?" Toledo said, an unpleasant snigger twisting his face. Then he pointed an accusing finger at Michael Scot and roared, "My power is *your* power, lest you forget, old man! This is *my* time, not yours. And neither you nor a witless child will stand in my way!"

Michael Scot turned away in disgust. "From the four elements you were created," he said evenly, "and on the Day of Reckoning, to them you shall return."

Without warning, Toledo let fly a crescent-shaped knife. It spun through the night air towards the great wizard, who did not dodge or defend himself – he simply stared at the whirling blade, which now hung before him, as if time itself had stopped. *Clink*! It fell harmlessly to the ground.

"Begone!" cried Michael Scot. He breathed deeply and then blew a great, icy wind, so fierce that not even

Toledo the Shapeshifter could withstand it. In a blaze of light, he was gone.

High above, Marnie was keeping watch at her bedroom door. She wanted to make sure that Dad was well and truly asleep before she interrogated the shoebox creatures. She didn't want him to think that she'd started talking to herself.

"But how can we be sssure ssshe isss the Chosssen One?" whispered Ailsa the snake.

"None of her predecessors ever managed to wake us up, did they?" Edwin said reasonably.

Wolfgang wasn't convinced. "But can we *trust* her?"

"She seems a nice enough wee lassie," said Bruno.

Edwin took charge again. "We tell her nothing – yet." As Marnie closed her bedroom door, he added quickly, "When the clock strikes midnight, we play dead, all right?"

Marnie glared down at the toys. "OK, I want the truth!" she snapped crossly. "*Who* are you? *What* are you? *Who's the Chosen One?*" She looked puzzled for a second. "And how come you just woke up when *I* couldn't wake you...?"

Edwin spread his wings and began to explain. "Well, Master...er...it is a tale of *considerable* length and complexity."

"Just cut to the chase, Eddie," said Marnie. She was rapidly losing her temper.

"Well," said the eagle, "to begin at the beginning…"

The arms on Marnie's clock clicked round to midnight, Edwin gave an exaggerated yawn and the toys fell asleep, snoring loudly.

"No!" cried Marnie. "Stop, I command you!" She couldn't believe it – they'd done it again. And she still didn't know how to wake them.

Outside, the great wizard waited. He no longer looked powerful – instead, he seemed old, dejected and very weary. Sadly, he glanced up at the mansion block. "Sleep well, child," he murmured. "Your adventure's just beginning." Then he slowly walked away.

CHAPTER THREE

FIRST DAY

Perched high on a clifftop, the dark fortress overlooked the raging sea beneath. Tantallon Castle – the home of Michael Scot. And deep underground in his Inner Sanctum, the great wizard had work to do. He strode across the room and grasped an ornate gold mask. At his touch, the mask began to creak, then juddered noisily into life. Beams of light shone brilliantly from between every panel.

Michael Scot placed the mask on his head. At once, it was as if all obstacles between Tantallon Castle and Marnie's flat had faded away. He used his new eyes to watch as…

…Marnie looked grumpily at herself in the mirror. Red jacket, yucky tartan tie and kilt, boring white shirt, sensible shoes… "What a geek," she said. She'd never looked *this* out of place in Denver – there, she'd been almost cool.

"Hurry up, Marnie!" called Dad. "You won't have time for breakfast."

Marnie took a last look at her totally uncool self before leaving the room. She locked the door behind her – she wasn't taking any more chances with toys that misbehaved.

Dad was on the phone again. "OK, fine. We'll come and collect it this evening," he said.

"Who was that?" asked Marnie when he'd put the phone down.

"It was about your birthday present from Grandma and Gramps – they tried to deliver it…" Dad quickly checked his watch. "Now, are you ready to go?"

"Erm, yeah," spluttered Marnie through a mouthful of cereal. "Just give me a sec – I've got to get my bag. Anyway, stop fussing," she said, "it's *me* that should have first-day nerves, not you!"

While she'd been out of the room, the occupants of the shoebox had been busy – apart from Wolfgang, that is. He'd flatly refused to try and escape again, grumbling that he was exhausted from yesterday's bid for freedom.

"Don't you know what he'll *do* to us?" said Edwin, teetering on the edge of the shoebox.

Wolfgang stretched out his paws and calmly went back to sleep.

"Oh, I'm not waiting for you!" Edwin jumped onto the bedside table and ushered Bruno towards

23

the edge. "My dear fellow, *après vous*," he said politely.

"No, please...after *you*," said Bruno.

Edwin peered nervously down from the bedside table. Ailsa had wasted no time and was already waiting far, far below on Marnie's bed. He leaned a little further and – with some help from Bruno's elbow – the metal eagle somersaulted onto the bed.

Bruno stifled a giggle and dived after him. "Wheeeeeeeee!" he yodelled. Then he said nervously, "Ohhhh. Wh-wh-what's that?"

An enormous teddy bear with scraggy fur and black beady eyes was towering over them.

"He's not moving," whispered Bruno. "Maybe he's asleep..."

"Then why, pray tell, are his eyes open?" Edwin said cleverly.

"*Because I am watching you!*" boomed Michael Scot's voice.

"Come on!" yelled Edwin, leading the charge towards the edge of the duvet.

Too late to slow down, they all tumbled off the bed and into Marnie's backpack – just as Marnie whisked it away.

Dad pulled up outside the grey, forbidding school just as the last stragglers were running through the gates.

"Great," said Marnie gloomily. "So now I'm walking in super-mega-late and everyone's going to stare at me."

"Maybe if we'd left when I said…" began Dad.

"And maybe if we'd stayed in Denver," Marnie snapped back, "I would still be in grade school and wouldn't have to go to this stupid Dumbsville—"

"That'll do, Marnie," said Dad, trying to remain calm. "Now why don't I come in with you and explain?"

Marnie looked at him, speechless. Did he know *nothing*? Didn't he realise that if she walked in with her dad, her reputation would be in tatters before she'd even opened her mouth? She might be new to this country, but she wasn't new to school. "Yeah, you can, like, hold my hand all the way to the classroom!" she said, grabbing first her bag and then the door handle.

Now Dad was angry too. "Just hold it right there, young lady!" he said, then softened his voice. "Maybe I was wrong to bring us to Scotland, but we're here now, so let's try, let's just really *try* to make it work."

In reply, Marnie yanked open the car door, slammed it loudly and then stomped across the playground.

Dad sighed.

And Toledo watched from the back seat of his chauffeur-driven car. He looked highly amused by what he'd seen.

"So, where to now, sir?" asked McTaggart, glancing apprehensively in the rear-view mirror.

Toledo flipped open a shiny compact mirror and admired his reflection. "Did I say we were going *anywhere*, McTaggart?" he asked smoothly. With a cruel smile, he snapped the compact shut.

★

Marnie hurried along the corridor, peering into classroom after classroom, looking desperately for any clue as to where she should be, when… Ow! "Hey, look where you're going!" she shouted at the small, brown-haired girl who'd walked into her.

"Sorry, didn't mean to… I was looking the other way," explained the girl. "You're new, right?"

"Is it *that* obvious?" Marnie sighed.

"Well, unless you're some kind of brainbox who's taking their exams early, you're in totally the wrong part of the school," said the girl, a friendly smile lighting up her freckly face.

"So can you tell me where to find…" – Marnie fumbled in her bag, pulling out a crumpled letter – "…Ms McKay's class?" she asked.

"You say it Mc-EYE," the girl said helpfully. "And that's my class. You'll have to get rid of that bag first though. You got a locker key?"

Marnie gritted her teeth and shook her head. This was turning into the sort of bad dream where you *never* got where you were going, no matter how hard you tried.

"Here," the girl said, handing over a small key. "Borrow mine – it's number fourteen. The lockers are down there and Ms McKay's just through there." She pointed down a smaller corridor and then waved her hand vaguely in the opposite direction. "I'll tell her you got lost, if you like."

"Hey, I can tell her myself, OK?" said Marnie

touchily. She didn't need anyone to stand up for her – she was perfectly capable of looking after herself.

The girl rolled her eyes and walked off. "I thought Yanks were supposed to be *friendly*," she muttered.

Marnie poked the key into the lock and swung open the door. But, as she heaved the backpack into the locker, she heard noises that sounded suspiciously like disobedient toys who would *not* stay home.

She whizzed open the zip and looked crossly into her backpack. "What are *you* doing here?" she demanded. Edwin, Ailsa and Bruno peered back sheepishly. "Were you trying to escape *again*?" Then she noticed that someone was missing. "Hey, where's Wolfgang–"

"There you are," interrupted a new voice.

Marnie quickly slammed the locker door shut and whirled round to face a smartly-dressed woman with red hair. "Hello, Marnie," she said. "I'm Ms McKay, your class teacher. Welcome to Marchmont School. Now, *your* locker's over there." To Marnie's dismay, Ms McKay opened the locker again and pulled out Marnie's backpack. "Goodness me, this is heavy. What have you *got* in here?" she exclaimed.

"Oh, just stuff," mumbled Marnie, taking her backpack from the teacher.

"Here you are," said Ms McKay, pointing to another locker. "Now, I believe you've already met Laura. Well, we'll soon have you introduced to everybody else."

Marnie turned the key and, as she moved to follow

27

her new teacher, spotted the number on her locker door. It was eleven.

Ms McKay burst into the classroom just as a full-scale riot was about to take place. "All right, everybody, quieten down!" she said loudly. "Now, I want you all to give a warm welcome to Marnie McBride."

The teacher's announcement was greeted with a smattering of applause. Marnie looked warily around the class – all she could see were unfriendly faces. How would she ever fit in here?

"Now, Marnie," Ms McKay said, "you'll be pleased to know that you're not the only new student here today. We've also got John Roberts." She waved her hand towards a tall, good-looking boy with longish, dark hair. He was lounging against the teacher's desk. "John, you were about to introduce yourself…?"

"Like to know why I got chucked out of my last school?" John Roberts began, with the laid-back confidence of a chat-show host. He spoke in an English accent that was as out of place in this classroom as Marnie's American voice. "Smoking in the bogs? Blowing up the science lab? No way, José. The headmaster of my school was *jealous* of me…"

"Yeah, right," jeered a boy at the back of the class.

"Seriously," John continued, adjusting his cuffs. He wore a strange ring that caught the light. "He used to do these really dumb party tricks every open day. The problem was…I could do them better." And with that, he pulled a long, silky scarf from his pocket and ran

it expertly through his hands. As if by magic, he now held a perfect egg between his fingers.

The pupils clapped admiringly. Ms McKay looked sympathetically at Marnie, as John sauntered to his seat. "Well, that's a tough act to follow, Marnie," the teacher said, "but perhaps you'd like to say something?"

Marnie took a deep breath. "Um, well…um, I'm at this school because my dad got a job over here. He's Scottish, right? In the beginning, I didn't really want to come because I liked things just fine back home… but my mom, well, she…"

"Perhaps you'd like to tell us about Denver?" said Ms McKay in a kind voice.

"Well, we've got lots of parks and sunshine," Marnie said, remembering the home she'd left behind. "Denver's like this *really* cool place."

"You're saying Edinburgh's *uncool*, then?" said one boy tetchily.

"That's enough, Stewart," warned Ms McKay.

Marnie gritted her teeth. She'd show them. "We've got enormous buildings like you've never seen," she continued, her voice growing louder and angrier. "And we've got killer snakes and bears that'll rip your guts out! What have *you* got?"

"OK, that'll do, Marnie," Ms McKay said quickly, as John Roberts began to clap slowly and mockingly. "Why don't you go and sit down there, behind Laura? We're just about to watch a slide show."

The teacher flipped the blinds shut, plunging

the room into inky blackness. Marnie felt totally deflated. Now everyone thought she was a show-off. She doubted she'd ever feel at home here.

The projector whirred into life, a photograph of Notre Dame Cathedral in Paris filled the screen.

"Who can tell me what kind of architecture this is?" Ms McKay asked.

Marnie saw a paper pellet whizz past and hit Laura on the back of the neck.

"It's Gothic, Miss," drawled John Roberts.

A paper pellet pinged Marnie's head and she winced. She wasn't impressed with her new classmates – they were *so* immature.

The slide projector clicked onto the next slide, this time of the Edinburgh cathedral. "Now, in St Giles' Cathedral, we have our very own example of the same architectural style. Perhaps you could fill us in, John?"

John nodded obligingly. "Well, it was originally built, around the 1120s, as a chapel for the relics of St Giles. Then the English burnt it down in 1370, no… it was 1385. That's it…1385." Suddenly, he stopped speaking and looked around in surprise. It was as if he'd forgotten where he was. "You really believe me?" he said quickly. "I just made it up."

"*Oww!*" A paper pellet stung Marnie's earlobe and this time she couldn't help crying out. Totally incensed, she picked up a schoolbook and hurled it at Stewart and his sidekick – just as Ms McKay opened the blinds.

"Marnie!" gasped the teacher. "What do you think you're doing? And on your first day too!"

"Well, some…" Marnie didn't know what to do or what to say. She was hardly going to make any friends by telling tales, was she?

But she needn't have worried – Laura came to the rescue again. "It was Stewart and Dougie, Miss. They've been firing those stupid paper pellets again."

"I saw them too," added John. "Downright harassment, if you ask me…"

The bell rang for break and everyone scrambled to their feet. Marnie had never been so relieved to reach the end of a lesson.

But two pupils weren't going to escape so easily.

"All right, you two," said Ms McKay to Stewart and Dougie. "Stay *right* where you are."

CHAPTER FOUR

FRIEND OR FOE?

As the river of pupils gushed out of the classroom, Marnie found herself next to Laura. "Thanks a lot," she said gratefully. "You saved my life!"

"Don't thank me," Laura replied dreamily. "Thank that John Roberts."

"John?" asked Marnie. Had she heard Laura right? "He seems even more of a loser than Stewart and Dougie."

"He's seriously fit," said Laura.

"Like he works out a lot?" asked Marnie. Now she was really confused.

"Fit doesn't mean like muscles and stuff," Laura explained. "It means, you know, good-looking."

By now, they'd reached the bank of lockers. Marnie hurriedly gabbled her excuses. "Sorry – catch you later! There's something I've got to do."

"Bye…" Laura said to Marnie's retreating back.

★

Marnie waited until the corridor had cleared before wrenching open the locker door, only to find that Edwin, Bruno and Ailsa had hopped out of her backpack and were relaxing on the metal floor. "You're supposed to be asleep!" she said crossly.

"Well, if you can't be bothered to learn the correct incantation…" Edwin said primly – and very loudly.

"Keep your voice down – this is a school!" hissed Marnie. A thought suddenly occurred to her. "But I guess you don't have schools wherever it is you're from," she added.

"I-I-I ," stammered Edwin, "I-I hope you are not implying that we are *uneducated*!" He puffed out his chest so much that Marnie was afraid he'd pop.

Ailsa flicked her forked tongue. "*Au contraire* – we're ssstudents like yoursssself."

"Look, if somebody finds you here, they'll…" Marnie couldn't bear to think of the consequences. "I've *got* to get you to sleep," she hissed. "You've *got* to help me!"

"Promissse you'll wake usss up again?" said Ailsa.

"Cross my heart and hope to die!" said Marnie.

It was Bruno who came to the rescue. "I think you said: 'If I woke you up, I'll bet I can send you *back to sleep*'," he said.

"Are you *sure*?" Marnie said. "*Back to sleep*?" Almost before the words were out of her mouth, they were lifeless – Edwin with one wing stretched out regally, Bruno ready to pounce and Ailsa curled into a slithering spiral.

Wham! In the time it takes a flash of lightning to stretch from cloud to earth, a very angry Stewart had pinned Marnie against the lockers – and Dougie had whipped the models from under her very nose. "Hey, give those back!" she shouted.

Dougie waved Bruno just out of Marnie's reach.

She lunged desperately for the bear, but Stewart held her tightly. "Tell us where you got them – and we'll give them back," he said.

"I found them in a junk shop," said Marnie sullenly. She could afford to give this secret away to Stewart and Dougie – after all, she reasoned, the shop was now emptier than their stupid heads. "They were inside an old shoebox, right?"

"Marnie McBride and her poxy Shoebox Zoo," chanted Dougie.

"*Shoebox Zoo* – the coolest thing in Colorado!" said Stewart.

A voice sliced through the boys' laughter. "Give them back to her."

Marnie's rescuer was none other than the mysterious John Roberts. He was leaning casually against a nearby wall.

"I reckon he fancies her, Stewart," said Dougie, with a smirk. Stewart sniggered and pushed Marnie roughly to one side. Slowly, deliberately, he and Stewart began to walk towards the new boy.

"Give them back and nobody will get hurt," said John smoothly.

"What? You going to make me?" sneered Stewart.

"Yeah, come on," added Dougie.

John Roberts did not seem to be fazed in the slightest by this show of boy power. "Dearie me," he said lightly. "Do you think I really have time to waste on a couple of…chickens?"

Marnie watched, dumbstruck, as he whipped a chain from his pocket and swung it to and fro, to and fro, in front of Stewart and Dougie. They stared blankly at the chain and the dazzling ring that hung from it.

"Now, you're going to do anything I command, aren't you, my fine fellows?" said John.

"Yes, we are…" chanted Stewart and Dougie.

"Splendid. Then go and put Marnie's animals back in her locker."

A smile crept onto Marnie's face as she watched Dougie do exactly as he was told. She couldn't believe her eyes or her ears. Was John Roberts for real…? He spoke as if he was on stage, he knew far more than the average pupil and now he'd actually *hypnotised* her tormentors.

And the show wasn't over. "Now, I want you to cluck like chickens," said John. "But when you're back in the classroom, everything will be back to normal. Understood?"

Obediently, Stewart and Dougie clucked away, bending and flapping their arms as if they really believed that they wore feathers instead of school uniforms.

"Wow! Where did you learn to do that stuff?" asked Marnie incredulously.

"If I told you, you'd never believe me." John bent down beside Marnie's locker and peered inside. "You don't have any more of these guys, do you? Like a… wolf, perhaps?"

Marnie froze. How did John Roberts know about Wolfgang? He couldn't possibly know about the Shoebox Zoo, unless… Did he have something to do with the junk shop and its creepy owner?

"I'm sure I've seen them before," he continued. "Yes…in a stained-glass window in St Giles'. And there was definitely a wolf too." He stared right at Marnie, as if looking into her very soul. "Where did you *really* get them? Not in a junk shop, I'll wager."

With a false smile, Marnie slammed her locker shut. "If I told you, you'd never believe me," she said sweetly. As far as she was concerned, John Roberts spoke like an adult, waved his hands like an actor and knew more facts than a quizmaster. He might be seriously fit, but he was seriously weird too. And she didn't trust him one bit.

"I want some answers – and I want them now!" stormed Marnie, emptying Edwin, Bruno and Ailsa from her backpack onto her bed and plucking Wolfgang from his resting place in the shoebox.

"Answers to what?" asked Edwin.

"Like, what you're doing in a stained-glass window in St Giles' Cathedral?"

"Who told you that?" said Ailsa slowly.

Marnie was beginning to lose her cool. Why couldn't these stupid toys give a straight answer to a question? Why were they always trying to wriggle away from the truth? Absent-mindedly, she grabbed her old teddy bear – at least there was one toy that wouldn't answer back. Instantly, the shoebox creatures shrank back in fear.

Marnie was momentarily baffled, before she realised that they thought her teddy was a *real* bear. She suppressed a giggle and decided to keep this information to herself – especially if it meant that they'd tell her more…

"All right, all right, we'll tell you anything you want to know," Bruno said in a quivering voice. "Only, please, keep that ferocious monster away!"

Wolfgang began. "Once, a long time ago, we were students of the great wizard…Michael Scot."

"You were *humans*?" Marnie was stunned. She wasn't sure what she'd expected – batteries or maybe an intricate clockwork mechanism? – but it sure wasn't this.

"Aye, and then he imprisoned us," said Bruno softly.

"Yes, turned us into our present – some might say *inappropriate* – form, and sent us to sleep," added Edwin, stretching wide his mismatched metal wings.

Ailsa continued the sorry tale. "Ssslumbering through war and flood, plague and famine, imprisssoned, lifeless across the centuriesss…"

"But how could he be so *cruel*?" demanded Marnie.

The animals looked at each other sheepishly. Bruno spoke. "Because we stole—"

"Lost!" interrupted Wolfgang. "Because we *lost* his Book."

"And until it is found," hissed Ailsa softly, "we will not regain our human form."

There was a loud knock. Marnie had just enough time to send the toys back to sleep before her bedroom door swung open. "Raaaarrrr!" she growled.

Dad looked into the room to see his daughter playing innocently with her blue and gold model wolf. "Shall we go and collect that parcel?" he asked, frowning.

"Just give me a sec!" said Marnie brightly. Great — now Dad thought she was a real baby for playing with toys... But at least he hadn't witnessed her Shoebox Zoo in action. Anything was better than that.

Inside the sumptuously, yet plainly decorated clock tower of the Balmoral Hotel, Toledo was using his incredible powers of concentration...to connect.

His task complete, Toledo's eyes snapped open. "I know where she is," he said. "She's about to collect another birthday present — one from across the great ocean that will give her vision as well as power. One she *must not have*."

McTaggart looked blank. "But your Excellency, I don't...er...understand what—" Before he could utter another word, Toledo's slender hands were wrapped round the chauffeur's throat.

"Make ready the car, fool!" Toledo bellowed. "*Rapido!*"

And far away, in a bitterly cold dungeon, someone else was watching Marnie, through the eyes of a golden mask that pulsed with light.

"Give me the eyes," breathed Michael Scot.

A feeling of drowsiness washed through Marnie's mind and she felt the irresistible urge to curl up and sleep. For a moment, it was as if the parcel depot had vanished and she was somewhere else entirely. It was the strangest feeling.

"There you go," said the courier, handing Marnie a tattered parcel. "Sorry, I had to open it," he explained. "Security and all that – it was playing merry hell with our X-ray machine… So you're the birthday girl, are you?"

Marnie nodded, grasping the parcel gratefully. She examined the torn wrapping and wondered if the courier would mind if someone ripped opened *his* presents before he'd seen them. In fact, so intent was she on the parcel from America that she did not see the large box travelling along the conveyor belt, or the tall, white-clad figure unfolding himself from inside that box. He loomed closer and closer to Marnie, reaching greedily towards her until…

Bam!

As Toledo crashed into an invisible barrier that

separated him from Marnie, it was as if the air itself shivered. Expressions of shock and rage flew across his face before he collapsed weakly back into the cardboard box. Swiftly, a courier stepped forward, taped the container shut and hurled it into the back of a waiting van. And, if Marnie *had* been looking, she might have recognised the silvery-haired courier – for he looked very like the owner of a certain junk shop…

"Are you not going to open it?" asked Dad.

Her fingers tingling with anticipation, Marnie flashed him a quick smile before ripping off the remaining wrapping paper to reveal a carved, wooden box. Inside was a beautiful silver pendant in the shape of a feather.

"It used to be your mother's," said Dad. "She wanted you to have it."

Marnie put the pendant round her neck, her lip quivering with the effort of holding back tears. "How does it look?" she asked quietly.

Dad gave her a wistful smile. "It looks beautiful, sweetheart," he replied.

CHAPTER FIVE

ECHOES OF THE PAST

our hooded figures crept silently along a dark passage. One held a lantern that split the gloom, casting long shadows behind them. There, at the end of the passage, lay the precious object they all sought – the Book. It was a weighty tome, bound in leather and decorated with gold and strange markings.

One of the four picked up the Book, but someone was there to stop them. That someone was tall and slender. He wore a cruel expression – and a brilliant white cloak. On his finger gleamed an elaborate ring. The four hooded figures turned and ran, taking the Book with them, while all around there echoed a woman's voice. "Marnie," she called. "Marnie!" An ominous banging grew louder and louder until–

Marnie woke up with a start, breathing heavily.

Dad was rapping at her bedroom door. "Wakey, wakey, sleepyhead," he called. "You don't want to be late for school on your second day as well."

"OK, OK…I'm coming," groaned Marnie. As she sat up in bed, she felt a strange tingling sensation at her throat. Marnie's fingers flew there and then she heaved a sigh of relief. It was just her feather pendant – she must have been lying on it.

Now she glanced around the little attic room, wondering when it would really begin to feel like *her* room. Her gaze settled on the shoebox and she grinned determinedly. If *she* was awake, it was time *they* were awake too. In a flash, Marnie had whipped off the lid and tipped the Shoebox Zoo onto the bed in front of her. "Awake, awake! I command you!" she said fiercely.

Nothing happened.

"What was it…?" muttered Marnie. She tried again. "Awake, awake…for I am your master."

Edwin stretched his wings and yawned.

Marnie had no time for polite greetings. She wanted the truth – and she wanted it now. "Tell me about the Book!" she demanded.

"Er…what-what-what Book?" asked Edwin innocently.

"The leather and gold book that I saw in my dream," snapped Marnie. "Could that possibly be the Book that you guys lost?"

"What else did you see?" growled Wolfgang.

"Four people, four *students* maybe, taking this Book and running away," said Marnie. "Someone terrible was chasing after them."

The creatures moaned in despair, as if Marnie's dream brought back bad memories for them.

"So it *was* you guys in my dream!" she said in triumph.

"I beg your pardon," said Edwin, promptly changing the subject, "but I think you'll find that *that* belongs to *me*."

"What?" Marnie said.

"*That*," said Edwin, "is my feather."

"It is not your feather," Marnie said sadly, clutching her pendant. "It was my mother's."

"That feather comes from right here," said Edwin, whirling round and sticking his bottom in the air. "Look!" Four shiny tail feathers glinted in the morning light, but there was a gap to show where a fifth feather had once been. The feathers matched Marnie's pendant exactly. "Your mother is a thief!" snapped Edwin.

Marnie gulped and tried to ignore the wave of sadness that threatened to overwhelm her. "My mother is dead…" she said quietly.

There was silence as all four of the shoebox creatures hung their heads.

"We're ssso ssssorry," hissed Ailsa softly. "We didn't know."

"We've been asleep for so long," explained Wolfgang.

"And she was only a wee girl like yourself when we saw her last," added Bruno.

Marnie could hardly believe her ears. "You *knew* her?" she asked, her eyes wide.

Wolfgang looked at Bruno crossly. "To say that we knew her would be an overstatement," he said.

"So you *saw* her, but you didn't *know* her," said Marnie, her voice growing louder as she got angrier. She'd had just about enough of these infuriating animals and their time-wasting tactics. "So, did you *talk* to her?"

But at that moment, there was another knock at the door. "For goodness sake, will you hurry up, Marnie!" shouted Dad.

"OK, I'm coming!" called Marnie. She scowled at the Shoebox Zoo — they needn't think that they were off the hook. Boy, did they have some explaining to do — especially now that she knew they'd at least *seen* her mother. "And until we get this sorted out," she said, in her most threatening voice, "you guys are coming with me."

The very last *dings* of the school bell were echoing as Marnie rushed through the empty corridors and up the stairs to her classroom.

"Hurry!" gasped Laura, who was a couple of steps higher. "We'll be late!"

"I wish I didn't have to be here at all," said Marnie glumly.

"Can you do that in America — just decide not to go to school?" asked Laura, with a glint in her eye. "Don't they have detention there…?"

The school bell rang again. "Now we really *are* late!" said Laura anxiously, pounding up the stairs. But as she and Marnie reached the top, the doors flew open and a crowd of their classmates rushed out.

"Order, order. Everybody stay calm," drawled John Roberts, looking directly at Marnie. "I'm afraid we have some bad news. There's a small…er…problem with the school's heating system. Regrettably, we get the day off." He brushed past her and carried on down the stairs.

Laura stared at Marnie in disbelief. "Wow," she breathed. "Do you always get what you wish for?"

Deep in thought, Marnie followed Laura down the stairs, down corridors packed with delighted pupils and back into the real world. Could she really have broken the school's heating system with one random wish? This was either the biggest coincidence ever or something totally creepy was going on.

"You must have special powers or something," said Laura, as if reading her mind. She nudged Marnie and winked at her. "But what's *really* weird is John Roberts always coming to your rescue. Maybe he fancies you."

Marnie couldn't help but laugh, sure now that her mind was playing tricks on her. Of *course* their day off was a coincidence.

"Hey, want to go down Princes Street?" said Laura. She laughed at Marnie's blank expression. "You know, shopping? Or don't they do that in Denver, Colorado? Come on – it'll be a laugh!"

Marnie laughed as Laura dragged her across the park. And, behind them, a white car glided to a halt beside the pavement. The rear window slid down and Toledo watched thoughtfully as the girls disappeared into the distance.

ɪn hallowed halls

"**h**ey, it's the cathedral – the one McKay showed us in class!" exclaimed Marnie, looking up at the huge, ornate building that towered above them. "Do you want to take a look?"

Laura looked at her new friend in amazement. "What about the shops? What are you now – a tourist?" she asked, as if this competed with murderer for the prize of 'most despicable job title'.

"No," said Marnie, smiling broadly, "I'm just a weirdo from Denver, Colorado." She looped an arm through Laura's and together they walked under the great stone arch.

Inside, it was cool, dark and silent. They walked slowly down the aisle, gazing up at the high, arched ceiling and around at the ancient carvings and tapestries.

"Are we looking for something?" Laura whispered.

"A stained-glass window," Marnie whispered back.

Laura glanced up at the many windows that

47

twinkled down at them. "Good place to find one—"

Suddenly, the cathedral's organ thundered into life, blasting their eardrums with sound. In total shock, Marnie and Laura stared towards the organ and spotted someone wearing their school uniform. With a flourish, the boy played the last notes and lifted his hands from the keys.

It was John Roberts.

"Fascinating old pile, isn't it?" he said cheerfully, walking towards Marnie and Laura. They looked at him in astonishment.

"The dean lets me practise here," explained John. He gave a small laugh. "He thinks I'm something of a child prodigy. That's why I know so much about our great cathedral – and your Shoebox Zoo window, of course. Come with me, ladies – I have something to show you."

John led Marnie and Laura under a low archway and into a magnificent chapel. Intricate wooden carvings covered the walls and rich tapestries hung from the ceiling. Suddenly, sunlight shone through a round, stained-glass window, instantly bathing the entire room in colourful light.

The stained-glass window! Marnie looked up – *there* was her Shoebox Zoo! Illuminated in brilliant reds, blues and golds were an eagle, a bear, a snake and a wolf. "Wow!" she said.

Laura squinted up at the window. "I guess it looks a bit like your Shoebox Zoo," she said. Everyone knew about Marnie's Shoebox Zoo, thanks to Stewart and Dougie.

"Curiously, all the other windows date from the Victorian era," said John knowledgeably. "But this one is centuries older. No one knows where it came from…"

"What do you think it means?" asked Laura.

"Some people say that the creatures are symbolic," John explained. "The eagle is the proud protector; the bear is loyal and true; the snake is stealthy and calculating, and the wolf the cunning provider. Others say that they're on a mission – a quest, if you like – searching for something."

Marnie stared hard at him, longing to know what lay behind his smug expression. "Like what?" she asked.

John gestured towards the stained-glass window. "I don't know…the eagle's looking for humility, the snake needs to learn trust, the bear lacks self-confidence and the wolf…why the wolf? Ah yes, he's looking for a lost father." He faced Marnie suddenly, looking at her with dark, piercing eyes. "We always search for the things we don't have."

Marnie stared back at him, suddenly uncomfortable. But now John was all smiles once more. "Fancy a guided tour, ladies?" he asked politely.

"OK," agreed Laura, who looked thoroughly bored of the decorated chapel.

But Marnie hung back. "Er…you guys go ahead," she said. "I'm going to take a closer look at the window."

Like an old-fashioned gentleman, John offered Laura
his arm and they left, leaving Marnie alone.

One by one, Marnie took the toy animals out of
her backpack, carefully standing them on a stone
ledge beneath the stained-glass window. Quickly, she
whispered the magic words: "Awake, awake, for I am
your master!"

Blinking in the coloured light, the Shoebox Zoo
gazed in awe at the stained-glass window – all except
Wolfgang, whose eyes flicked to and fro as if he sensed
someone watching them.

"Oh, a very fine likeness," said Edwin proudly,
"although maybe they haven't *quite* done justice to
my beak…"

"But what are we doing there?" asked Bruno.

"That's what *I'd* like to know…" said Marnie,
frowning expectantly at the four creatures.

"Now, this is a very special place," said John, pointing to
a dark, wooden door that lay at the foot of a short flight
of steps. He opened a creaky gate at the top of the steps.
"Not many people get to see it. Care to take a look?"

"Really?" asked Laura nervously, slowly walking
down the stone steps.

"Haddo's Hole," said John. "It's where all the
heretics and witches were kept. They could scream for
hours and no one would ever hear them."

Laura looked back. "Are you not coming?" she
asked, her voice trembling slightly.

"I've already seen it – and I have to admit that it was too much for me," said John calmly. "I wouldn't blame you if you were *scared*."

Stung, Laura dragged open the wooden door and stepped bravely inside. From his vantage point at the top of the steps, John Roberts gave a flick of his wrist – and the door slammed shut with a resounding thud. He smiled.

And as much as Laura pushed and rattled the door, it would not open. "That's not *funny*!" she shouted. "*Let me out!*"

Marnie's father wasn't having the best of days. First, he'd arrived late for work, colliding with a packed trolley of books and sending them flying – though he had found a very interesting book as he'd tidied away the mess. Then, he'd discovered a visitor in the restricted area of the University Library.

"Excuse me – can I help you?" said Mr McBride, pulling at the metal gate at the entrance to the section. It didn't budge. Briefly wondering how the old man in the old-fashioned tartan coat had managed to get inside, he unlocked the gate. "I'm afraid you're not allowed in here," he said. "You need a Special Collections pass. Do you have one?"

The man rummaged in his many pockets and eventually drew out a piece of card, which he thrust towards Mr McBride.

Marnie's father looked curiously at the ancient,

dog-eared library card in his hand. The name written there was *Michael Scot*. And the date was *11 November, 1811*.

Mr McBride frowned, scratched his head and then took the book he'd found back to his desk. He was slowly flicking through the pages of *When Bad Things Happen to Good Children* when he noticed that the man in the tartan coat was lurking nearby.

"Excuse me?" the old man said.

"Sorry," said Mr McBride, closing the book. "I'm a little worried about my daughter." And then things fell into place. "*That's* where I know you from," he said. "You're the one from the junk shop who gave my daughter those funny carved animals!"

The silver-haired man checked out the cover of Mr McBride's book and a look of concern crossed his face. "No, no…" he stammered. "You're thinking of someone else. I'm looking for a book – *The Gazetteer of Scottish Religious Architecture*, 1672."

"Oh," said Mr McBride. "That rings a bell," he murmured, before leading the man deep into the library to a bookshelf that was rarely visited.

Soon, they found the book that the old man was looking for. Mr McBride opened the front cover and chuckled. "Funny, this hasn't been checked out in a hundred and eleven years – and you're the second person to borrow it in a week!" He stamped the book and handed it over.

"Second person?" asked the man, a flicker of anxiety

in his eyes. Without waiting for an answer, he turned and hurried from the library, just as the chimes from an old clock began to sound.

"Remember, it needs to be back on the twenty-sixth!" called Mr McBride, before starting to read once more.

"…Ten…Eleven." Marnie counted the noisy chimes that echoed from the cathedral's bell tower. In the dead silence that followed, she felt an involuntary shiver run down her spine. She felt afraid, but she didn't know why.

Then the toys began to shake. "He's here!" groaned Edwin, hugging Ailsa in terror.

"Who's here?" whispered Marnie urgently.

"Toledo," growled Wolfgang. "The Shapeshifter."

The sound of distant footsteps echoed through the cathedral and Marnie looked up, feeling apprehensive. *Who* was Toledo? *Why* were Edwin and the others so terrified? And what was she going to *do*? Then she looked back at the stone ledge to discover that the Shoebox Zoo had gone.

"Ailsa!" called Marnie desperately, running from the chapel. "Wolfgang? Where are you?"

"Marnie? *Marnie!*" cried a muffled voice.

Marnie stopped in her tracks. "Laura?" she called. The voice seemed to be coming from a door at the bottom of some steps. She rushed down and slid back the heavy bolt that held it shut.

"What were you *doing* in there?" Marnie asked Laura, when she'd pulled open the door. "Hey, where's JR?"

"As if you didn't know!" spluttered Laura. She was absolutely, mind-blowingly furious.

"I don't!" said Marnie. "What are you talking about?"

"The little plan you two cooked up," Laura snarled. "Let's make a fool out of Laura! You guys go ahead – I want to check out a stained-glass window. Yeah, right!"

"What?" Marnie was stunned. "But I'm your friend – that's crazy!"

"Crazier than talking to a bunch of toy animals?" retorted Laura. "You and John Roberts are *both* weird!" Without waiting for a reply, she spun on her heel and stomped angrily towards the exit.

In another part of the cathedral, Wolfgang had been discovered by the very person that the Shoebox Zoo was trying to escape – Toledo. He loomed above the cowering wolf, a sly smile twisting his mouth. "You know why I am here," he said smoothly, "and you know what I want."

Wolfgang looked up at the Shapeshifter warily, then nodded his head.

Toledo leaned nearer. "Does the girl-child know for what she seeks?" he asked quietly, menacingly.

"Yes," growled Wolfgang.

Toledo brought his face so close to the wolf that

their noses were almost touching. "You and your foolish little friends will help her find it, won't you?" he whispered. "And you will say nothing of our little encounter?"

Wolfgang nodded enthusiastically.

Toledo smiled to himself. "What do you want, my treacherous little Wolfie, hmm? To be human again? Oh, not just that, surely… Power? Revenge?"

An expression of pure longing swept across Wolfgang's face.

"Be careful what you wish for," said a bitter voice. And Michael Scot stepped from the shadows, brandishing his staff.

Toledo vanished in a flash of light and reappeared on the opposite side of the cathedral. He threw out his arm, hurling a stream of fizzing, flashing energy towards Michael Scot and knocking the staff out of his hands. The wizard blocked the energy surge with one hand and deflected it back at Toledo.

And then began a great struggle for power. Shafts of light blasted to and fro, crackling in the still air of the cathedral until…slowly…Toledo started to take control. Michael Scot weakened – the battle was draining his energy, little by little. Forced backwards by Toledo, the wizard edged across the stone floor, slowly sinking to his knees beside a huge, brass candlestick.

Michael Scot was nearly spent, his old face showing the strain he was under. With one last effort, he reached out a hand and grasped the candlestick. At once,

Toledo's deadly energy flowed through the wizard's body to the candlestick and then harmlessly down to the floor. Then it was over.

Quickly summoning his staff, which sprung into the air towards him, Michael Scot aimed it at Toledo and sent one last bolt of energy towards his enemy. Spectacularly, the Shapeshifter shattered into tiny pieces and crumbled to the floor.

Toledo's chauffeur appeared from behind a stone column. "Eleven hundred pieces, is it, sir?" he asked. He watched disapprovingly as Michael Scot drank greedily from a tiny crystal bottle as if his life depended on it.

"Count each piece eleven times and your loathsome Shapeshifter shall return," the wizard sneered nastily. "It's not the Day of Reckoning yet, McTaggart. Only then can I hope to destroy him."

McTaggart flinched from the wizard's words, then bent down and started to count the white pieces of stone that covered the floor. "Don't worry, your maliciousness," he murmured. "I'll have you out of here in no time – every little piece."

Someone else had witnessed the battle. "Finally," growled a tiny voice. "It's taken you eleven centuries to do something for me."

Michael Scot looked down at the blue and gold wolf that crouched nearby. His expression was unreadable. "You're playing a very dangerous game," he warned.

★

Marnie sat on a pew in the decorated chapel, feeling tired, dejected and utterly alone. Then an eagle, a bear and a snake pattered towards her.

"He's gone," said Edwin in a relieved voice.

But Marnie wasn't interested. "Yeah, well, *he's* not the only one, whoever *he* is. I had *one* friend in that stupid school and now she thinks that… Oh, it doesn't matter." Her shoulders drooped.

"You've got us," said Bruno. "We're your friends."

"But you keep running away, don't you?" Marnie pointed out.

"No, no…" said Edwin. "We didn't run away – we made a strategic withdrawal."

"From *who* exactly?" asked Marnie.

"From Toledo," replied Wolfgang, stepping out from behind a pillar. "The Shapeshifter. Juan Roberto Montoya de Toledo, to be precise. A wizard – the nemesis of Michael Scot."

"Nemesis, shemesis," muttered Edwin.

Marnie sighed. "Please don't tell me this has something to do with your stupid Book too. I mean, shouldn't there be clues?" She was suddenly thoughtful. "The window… It should tell us something."

As she spoke, a single sunbeam illuminated a shape *behind* the figures in the stained-glass window.

"Hey, there's a castle in it!" exclaimed Marnie.

"It's…it's Tantallon," said Bruno.

Ailsa hissed. "Home of Michael Scot."

"Where we used to live," sighed Wolfgang wistfully.

Edwin gazed up at the window. "Where the Book was stol–" Wolfgang elbowed him. "Where the Book was *lost*," Edwin corrected himself.

"Well, why didn't you tell me that in the first place?" said Marnie, smiling to herself. Perhaps they were getting somewhere at last.

CHAPTER SEVEN

A GUIDE FOR THE PERPLEXED

"**O**K, now for the fun part," said Marnie, wiggling her mouse experimentally. "We're going on the Net…"

The Shoebox Zoo animals were gathered round her keyboard. They glanced at each other, as if she were talking a foreign language.

"The *Inter*net," said Marnie. They still looked blank. "It's like a big library, where you go to take out books, except you don't have to go. You can just stay here and…er…connect."

By now, the creatures were looking totally confused.

"Where have you *been*?" said Marnie.

"We told you already – *asleep*," said Wolfgang.

"So, no cars, no planes, no first man on the moon… according to you guys, we're still living in caves!" Marnie scoffed.

Edwin rattled his feathers importantly. "I hope

59

you're not suggesting that we are uncouth savages!"

"Well, let's face it, Eddie, you're not exactly at the cutting edge of technology." Marnie paused, her fingers in mid-air above the keyboard. "Michael Scot – is that one 't' or two?"

"One," replied Wolfgang.

"Wow! Your master *was* an important guy," breathed Marnie. There were thousands of listings for Michael Scot. She clicked on a link and began to read. "What's an alchemist?"

"You accuse *us* of ignorance and savagery and you don't even know what an *alchemist* is?" spluttered Edwin.

"An alchemist," interrupted Wolfgang, "is a kind of early scientist who specialised in changing base metal into gold. But that doesn't begin to describe Michael Scot."

Marnie scrolled down the website to reveal a photo of a ruined castle, perched high on a clifftop. "Tantallon Castle – said to be the seat of Michael Scot..." she read.

The shoebox creatures looked at the screen and gasped. Then they turned to Marnie, fear and awe in their eyes.

"Your power is mighty indeed, oh great Master," said Bruno.

"The battlementsss ssscaled," hissed Ailsa.

"The castle in ruins!" Wolfgang added.

Now it was Marnie's turn to be confused. What

were they talking about? But before she could ask, there was a loud knocking at the bedroom door. "Back to sleep!" she whispered.

"Marnie! How many times have I told you about locking the door?" said Dad, when she'd opened it. "Who were you talking to?"

"Nobody," replied Marnie quickly. "Just doing my homework."

Dad looked at the photo on the screen. "Hmm… Tantallon Castle…" he mused, before reciting aloud:

"'*Tantallon vast;*
Broad, massive, high and stretching far,
And held impregnable in war…'
That's what Scott said on the subject," he finished.

This caught Marnie's attention at once. "Michael Scot was a poet?" she asked.

"No, but Sir Walter Scott was." Dad rubbed his chin thoughtfully. "Although Michael Scot did write something, actually."

"He wrote a book?" asked Marnie, hardly able to contain her excitement.

"What's with the big interest in a twelfth-century alchemist?" said Dad, grinning at his daughter.

"Er…" Marnie scrabbled around for an excuse that Dad would believe *and* approve of. "Science!" she announced. "We're doing a project on early science."

"Well, I'm sure we've got a Michael Scot book in the University Library, but it's pretty dull and boring…" Dad looked unsure, but he couldn't ignore Marnie's

sparkling eyes. "I'll organise it for the weekend," he promised. "Now, don't stay up too late, OK? And *stop locking the door*."

That night, Marnie dreamt again…

A quill pen scratched strange shapes onto parchment, the pen held by a beautiful, slender hand. "Marnie," said a woman's voice, over and over. Four cloaked figures rushed past – one holding the Book. "Marnie, Marnie…" A figure in a white cloak followed the fleeing figures.

Marnie slept fitfully on.

At school the next day, only one person bothered to speak to her – and it wasn't Laura.

"Hello, Marnie!" called John Roberts, as he breezed into the classroom, settling himself at the back of the room.

Marnie pretended she hadn't heard him.

By lunchtime, she was heartily sick of being ignored. Laura would come nowhere near her and looked the other way when Marnie smiled anxiously in her direction. And Marnie had no one else to talk to. She was eating her sandwiches in the dining hall when John Roberts entered, flanked by his brand-new fans, Stewart and Dougie.

Marnie noticed that Laura was leaving the room. "Laura, please!" she called.

Slowly, Laura turned round. She was flushed and angry and looked in no mood to talk.

"Just listen, will you?" pleaded Marnie. "I didn't know that John Roberts was going to be at the cathedral. He gatecrashed the whole thing. As for that dungeon he locked you in…I had nothing to do with it." She glanced anxiously at Laura – was she softening? "And I sure don't want to lose you as a friend because of that jerk," she finished.

Laura seemed uncertain. "So you didn't want me out of the way so you and he could…"

"Please!" Marnie grimaced. "You're the one who said he was cute, not me."

"I said he was weird, not cute," said Laura. "He is seriously strange. I mean, one minute he's teacher's pet…"

"And the next he's, like, this really annoying loser," finished Marnie.

"So why was he so keen to get you on your own?" asked Laura.

"How should I know?" said Marnie. It was true – she was pretty sure John Roberts didn't fancy her, so why did he insist on turning up everywhere she went?

"Talking about me again?" said a familiar voice.

Laura took one look at the immaculately dressed schoolboy and stalked off.

"Aww…I just came over to apologise," said John. His tone was entirely unrepentant. "Oh, well. You can't say I didn't try."

Marnie whirled to face him. "Look, locking somebody up in a weird dungeon and freaking them

out is *not* going to make you flavour of the month, right?" she shouted. "And if you think that you and I have some special relationship because we just happened to arrive at this stupid school on the same day, you are seriously mistaken, OK?"

Marnie hurried after Laura, hoping that there was time to catch her before the next lesson. She didn't notice that she'd forgotten her lunchbox.

By the time Marnie reached the classroom and slipped into the seat behind Laura, Ms McKay was already talking about the school trip.

"Now, the only conditions are that it must be in or near Edinburgh. And," the teacher said, ignoring Stewart's raised hand, "it must be of historical or scientific interest."

Stewart shrugged and lowered his hand as Marnie raised hers. Inside, she was bubbling with excitement. This was the chance she'd been waiting for – the chance to find out about the home of Michael Scot and the Shoebox Zoo. "I'd like to go to Tantallon Castle," she said.

Ms McKay surveyed the class, her eyes resting on John Roberts. "John, what about you?" she asked. "I'd have thought that a visit to Tantallon would be right up your street."

John examined his fingernails carefully before speaking in a scathing voice. "It's a long-forgotten, insignificant garrison on the fringes of the civilised world. It's hardly my idea of history."

"Well, I think we should take a vote on it," said Ms McKay.

Suddenly, Marnie felt an odd, prickling sensation, and then the world began to shift before her eyes. It was as if the classroom were moving in and out of focus. Everyday objects became strangely unreal – her desk, classmates, even Ms McKay. She glanced at the human skull sitting on a nearby shelf. Its empty eyes were gazing in her direction... It was watching her! Marnie gave herself a little shake – it was just an old skull from their science lessons. She tried desperately to concentrate on what the teacher was saying.

"For goodness' sake, lassie..." said the skull.

Marnie flinched and clutched her pendant, which suddenly seemed to be throbbing with energy. A quick glance around the room showed that no one else seemed to have heard the words.

"Tell them about the headless ghosts!" whispered the voice.

"What headless ghosts?" Marnie whispered back.

"Any old headless ghosts – use your imagination!" the voice snapped irritably.

Marnie sighed. As if voices in her head weren't enough, hers had to be cross voices... Suddenly, her pendant became cool metal in her hand once more and the world stopped swaying.

"Are you all right, Marnie?" asked Ms McKay.

"I–I just remembered the headless ghosts who haunt the castle dungeons. And the terrible twins –

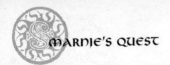

the ones who stole the king's gingerbread and were cruelly beheaded for it. Their cries can still be heard to this day…" Marnie was really getting into this now – and she knew exactly how to guarantee the trip to Tantallon. "Back home, we go on ghost hunts all the time. I guess you Scots are just too chicken."

"You want to bet?" snapped Stewart.

"We are voting, not betting!" Ms McKay called out. "Now, all those in favour of Tantallon…?"

One hand shot up, then another and another until a sea of hands waved in the air. Even Laura voted for the trip to Tantallon. Dougie too. The only hands to remain firmly on their desks belonged to a scowling Stewart and a *very* unhappy John Roberts.

CHAPTER EIGHT

AN UNEXPECTED GUEST

After school, Laura and Marnie strolled down the street together. The promise of a school trip had totally broken the ice. Yesterday's events suddenly seemed as if they'd happened years ago.

"You don't really believe in ghosts, do you?" asked Laura.

Marnie was silent, wondering if she should take the plunge. "What if I told you that I hear voices in my head?" she began cautiously.

"I'd say you were crazy…" replied Laura. Then she hesitated, realising that Marnie wasn't kidding. "So what are they like, these voices?"

Relieved that Laura wasn't rolling on the pavement in hysterics, Marnie tried to explain. "Well, I can't hear them this minute… Does that make me only half-crazy? There's this old guy – he spoke to me in class today."

"Wait!" said Laura, stopping dead in her tracks. "That's when you looked like you were going to faint, right?"

Marnie nodded. "And then there are these other little guys who I can see right in front of me…" She paused. Now Laura was giving her a *really* weird look – and she didn't blame her. Marnie took a deep breath. She knew what she had to do. "Look, my house is just round the corner – I'll show you."

Laura hung back.

"Hey, *I'm* the crazy one," Marnie joked. "It's not like it's catching or something!"

"Hiya, sweetheart!" said Dad as they walked through the door.

"Hi, Dad," said Marnie, quickly squeezing past him. "This is Laura."

Dad stretched out a hand to Laura and pumped her hand up and down. "Pleased to meet you, Laura. Come in, come in… You'll have tea with us, then?"

"OK…" Laura replied hesitantly.

"Pizza and Spanish sausage," Dad called after them, as they hurried off. "You're not vegetarian, are you?"

"No," replied Laura, following Marnie to her room.

Once inside, Marnie shut the door tight. "Sorry about my dad," she said, rolling her eyes. "He can be a little bit over the top sometimes…"

Laura looked slowly around Marnie's attic room,

taking everything in. Then she wandered over to the shelf and picked up the framed photo that Marnie gazed at every night before she slept and every morning when she woke. "Is this your mum?" she asked. "Where is she?"

Marnie gulped. This was the question that she dreaded above all others. "She's dead," she replied slowly, trying to keep the sadness she felt deep inside. "She died in Denver."

Laura's face fell. "Is that why you came to Scotland?"

"Kind of," said Marnie. "My dad had already been offered the job at the University Library. I guess he just decided to take it because he was so cut up about what happened to my mom." She swallowed. It was hard to think back to those terrible, dark days.

"Sorry, I shouldn't have asked," said Laura, replacing the frame on the ledge. She gave Marnie an encouraging smile. "So, when do I get to see these other…guys of yours?"

Relieved that Laura had changed the subject, Marnie locked the door. She whirled round to face Laura, who seemed a little spooked by the fact that Marnie was now acting like a secret agent. "I've got to be able to trust you," explained Marnie seriously. "So, do you swear to keep this a secret till the day you die?"

Laura gulped, then went for it. "OK…I swear," she said.

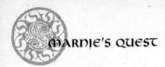

"Till the day you die?" prompted Marnie.

"Till the day I die…"

Marnie reached for the shoebox sitting on her bedside table and whispered, "Awake, awake, for I am your master."

And then the doorbell rang.

Never had a doorbell seemed so loud or rung for so long. Inexplicably, Marnie felt chilled…and very afraid. She unlocked her bedroom door with trembling hands and rushed down the hall, standing on tiptoes to peer through the spyhole. But before she looked, somehow she knew who it would be.

"Come on! Are you going to open the door or not?" called Dad from the kitchen. He strode along the hall and pulled the handle before Marnie could stop him.

"Hi," said the schoolboy who stood outside. "You must be Marnie's dad. I'm John Roberts —I'm in Marnie's class. She left this at school." He held out a lunchbox decorated with the Denver Broncos' logo.

"Well, that's very kind of you to deliver it personally," said Dad, taking the lunchbox.

Rather than turning to leave, John remained on the doorstep, looking expectant.

"Well, I'm just making tea…I'm sure Marnie would be delighted if you joined us. Isn't that right, sweetheart?" said Dad, ignoring the withering look that Marnie directed at him.

"Excellent pizza, Mr McBride," said John, as he

polished off the last of his meal. "Chorizo, wasn't it?"

Dad smiled broadly. "Hand-made from a secret recipe that's been handed down through the generations," he replied.

Marnie concentrated on clearing away the plates. She still had that nagging feeling that all was not right, that John's arrival had something to do with the Shoebox Zoo... Or was he just trying to wreck her friendship with Laura?

John smiled awkwardly at Marnie's dad. "Er...Mr McBride," he said, "I was just wondering if I could use the...er...facilities?"

Unable to contain herself, Marnie giggled. What was she thinking? John Roberts was no more dangerous than her Shoebox Zoo.

"Down the hall and on the left," said Dad helpfully.

"Most kind, Mr McBride," replied John.

John Roberts shut the kitchen door behind him and sniffed deeply. Then he made his way to Marnie's bedroom and slipped inside. Sniffing faster now, like an animal on the trail of a particularly strong scent, the schoolboy moved around the room, his gaze resting briefly on the empty bedside table. Then he smiled, spun round and walked swiftly to a white, painted wardrobe. John grasped the doorknob firmly and pulled. When the door did not open, he rattled the doorknob angrily. Still it remained shut.

Stepping back from the cupboard, the boy raised his arms majestically into the air and closed his eyes. At once, his arms began to grow longer, his fingers more elegant. He grew taller, leaner, older. His dark, curling hair vanished, his expression became more and more menacing until...John Roberts had transformed into Juan Roberto Montoya de Toledo – the Shapeshifter.

Toledo pointed a finger and the lock exploded in a puff of smoke. Now the door opened easily. He reached inside and casually plucked the shoebox from the cupboard where Marnie had hidden it.

"It's such a great pleasure to meet you all again, my little friends," sneered Toledo, emptying the carved animals onto the bed. They cowered in utter terror. Eagerly, the Shapeshifter reached for Wolfgang, but as he touched the little wolf, great blue sparks leapt between his fingertips and Wolfgang's wooden coat, crackling and flashing like a miniature electric storm.

"*Caramba!*" hissed Toledo, nursing his hand. "How could I forget *again*?"

While the Shapeshifter moaned in agony, the Shoebox Zoo took their chance-and scrambled towards freedom. Edwin, Bruno and Ailsa made it over the window ledge and onto the roof, but Wolfgang wasn't so lucky. Toledo blocked his escape route with the photo of Marnie's mother.

"Now, why does the girl-child want to go to Tantallon?" Toledo asked, in a dangerously quiet voice.

"She knows it's Michael's castle," growled Wolfgang.

"She must *not* come under the wizard's spell," hissed Toledo. "He will corrupt her totally. She must deliver the Book to *me*. And you, my little wolf, must help her."

By now, Marnie and Laura had helped to tidy and wash up and still John hadn't returned.

"Do you think he's flushed himself down the facilities?" said Laura, giggling. Marnie grinned back at her.

And at that exact moment, John walked back into the kitchen, looking flustered and a little out of breath. "Thank you for your hospitality, Mr McBride," he said hurriedly. "I've got to be off – lots of homework to be done. But…Marnie must come over to my place for tea some time. And Laura, of course. Er…I'll make my own way out." He left.

Marnie and Laura looked at each other in disbelief. *Who* mentioned homework in front of adults? *No one!* They gritted their teeth and waited for…

"Homework," said Dad sternly. "I'm driving Laura home right now."

Marnie walked into her room to find Wolfgang hauling the rest of the Shoebox Zoo back through the window. "Trying to escape again…?" she said.

"I know that'sss what it looksss like…" began Ailsa.

But Marnie was in no mood for excuses. She couldn't leave the Shoebox Zoo alone for five minutes without them making a run for it. "So what were you actually doing?" she asked. "Taking skydiving lessons?"

"Look, in truth, we *were* escaping – but not from you," said Edwin. "Toledo the Shapeshifter was right here. In your room. In the flesh. I swear it!"

"You tell her, Wolfgang," hissed Ailsa.

Wolfgang was silent for a few seconds before speaking. "The truth is…it was *you* we were escaping from," he snarled. "We all came to the same decision."

The other three creatures stared at Wolfgang, disbelief plastered across their faces.

"Which was what, Wolfgang?" Marnie said slowly. Just who was telling the truth here? Could she believe a single word that *any* of them uttered?

Wolfgang bared his teeth. "That you're a silly little girl and we have no use for you any more!" he barked.

Marnie lost her temper. "Oh yeah? Well, big deal!" she shouted. "Why would I need your help if I know where the Book is already?"

At this, Wolfgang looked horrified. But it was too late for apologies.

"So you can all go back to sleep!" finished Marnie.

On Saturday morning, Marnie's dad kept his promise and took her to the University Library. It was so early that the library was deserted. Together, they wandered through a labyrinth of shelves stacked floor to ceiling with books.

"Now, er…" muttered Dad, confusion crinkling his forehead. He turned down an aisle and was lost to sight.

"Dad?" said Marnie, staring into the shadows. Suddenly, she sensed that someone was watching her, and glanced over her shoulder. No one was there. But the feeling hadn't gone away. Marnie turned into another aisle and glimpsed a pair of legs on an upper level. It was…it was…Dad. She breathed a sigh of relief.

"Catch!" he called, throwing a book down to Marnie. To her disappointment, she saw that this was no weighty leather-bound tome, but a small, thin book bound in red velvet.

Marnie sat down at a nearby desk and opened the book. It was all gibberish – Greek, Latin, Spanish, Welsh…? All except for the index card inside the front cover. *A Guide for the Perplexed by Michael Scot*, it said.

"That's not the book you're looking for," said a voice.

Slowly, cautiously, Marnie raised her head, feeling a thrill of excitement flow through her. For, even though the opposite seat had been empty just a moment before, an old man with a craggy face now sat there. He wore an eager, yet incredibly weary expression. And he looked strangely familiar.

"There's a very interesting map on page eleven," he said quietly. "They say that some maps are guides for the feet, others for the imagination…"

"Hey," said Marnie, suddenly realising how she knew him. It was that weird old man who'd given her the Shoebox Zoo. "You're that guy from the junk shop, aren't you?" she asked.

He didn't answer. "Use the map," he repeated urgently, his brow furrowing. "Use your imagination… page eleven."

Marnie turned to page eleven and looked closely at the curious diagram that was printed there. It was a black circle, intersected by curvy white lines that bent and twisted towards a rectangular shape in the middle. What it was a map *of*, she had no idea. Marnie looked up to ask the man more, but the seat was now empty.

He'd gone – as quietly as he'd arrived.

CHAPTER NINE

TANTALLON CASTLE

"That's it, indubitably, the Inner Sanctum," announced Edwin to the rest of the Shoebox Zoo, studying the map in Marnie's library book. He pointed his wing. "And this white line shows the corridor down which we escaped."

Ailsa slithered around the book, which lay open on her desk. "It'sss all coming back to me," she hissed, swaying to and fro.

"OK, listen up," said Marnie, as she dashed into her bedroom. "I'm in enough trouble at school already, so if you guys step out of line on this trip, you are going to be in *even deeper*. You got that?" She really meant it. This trip was very important to her — she *had* to find out what the curious map showed. And she had a feeling that Tantallon Castle was just the place to do it.

"Just so that nobody is tempted to misbehave, you

are all going to bedibyes," Marnie said, smiling sweetly. "*Back to sleep.*"

The animals froze.

A strange idea crept into Marnie's mind. What if…? No, it was too ridiculous for words. But the idea wouldn't go away. *What if there was another way of controlling the Shoebox Zoo?* What if she could *will* them to obey her? She closed her eyes tightly, clenched her fists and concentrated really, really hard, so hard that it seemed she could feel energy zapping through her veins and fizzling at her fingertips.

The animals awoke. And Marnie stared at them in utter disbelief. She'd done it. She really had. She, Marnie McBride, had summoned the power that lay within her to perform actual *magic*.

"Make up your mind, lassie!" grumbled Edwin. "Do you want us *awake* or do you want us *asleep*?"

"Didn't you see what I did?" Marnie squeaked. "I woke you up just by *thinking* about it!"

Bruno turned to Edwin, wearing a wise smile. "See. I knew she was the Chosen One."

The coach had left the city far behind. It travelled over rolling hills and through leafy green valleys, heading towards the coast and Tantallon, where the ruined castle faced out over the treacherous sea.

"OK, everybody!" called Ms McKay, as the crowd of restless pupils gathered round her in the car park. She spoke sternly. "Now, this is an historic monument and I don't want any damage to be done to it – or to you. There are some areas that are marked 'private'. Anyone caught trespassing will be up in front of the Head in the morning. Is that clear?"

Ms McKay's grim warning had no effect whatsoever on Marnie – she was too busy gazing all around at the legendary castle. The crumbling battlements towered far above her, dark, brooding and magnificent. Sure, it might be a ruin, but it was a pretty cool ruin – and one she couldn't wait to explore.

Suddenly, an enthusiastic guide appeared, grinning widely. "Willie McTaggart at your service, lads and lassies!" he gushed, his eyes scanning the pupils carefully. "I'm here to tell you the history of Tantallon Castle. Now, although these walls are seven hundred years old, 'tis said that some parts of Tantallon are over eleven hundred years old." He chuckled to himself. "That's even older than me!"

High on Tantallon's battlements, a cloaked figure watched. "Let her get on with it," muttered the old man. "If she is who she pretends to be, she'll find her own way." He swirled his robes round him and vanished.

Meanwhile, realising that everyone was spellbound by the strange guide's words, Marnie took her chance and sneaked away. She glanced quickly at the map she had photocopied from the library book, then hurried inside the castle, passing the sign that said 'Private – dungeons' without a second glance.

By now, McTaggart had gathered Marnie's classmates round an old well. He spoke in a low, hypnotic voice. "As legend has it, 'tis down this very well that lies the magical Inner Sanctum of the great and powerful Michael Scot – some people call him wizard, but early scientist was his preferred title…or so I'm told."

Laura had seen Marnie leave out of the corner of her eye. Impulsively, she followed – and Stewart and Dougie weren't far behind. John Roberts watched them all go, an evil smile twisting his young face.

With tentative steps, Marnie made her way along the ancient hallway, away from the sunlight and nearer her goal. At least, she hoped so. She rounded a corner and found herself at the top of a spiral staircase when her pendant began to blaze with a searing heat and she saw…four figures hurtling from Tantallon Castle and across the courtyard, their cloaks flapping wildly behind them. A tall man in a dazzling white coat watched, his face closed and callous…

Then she was back. Marnie swayed, her breathing ragged, before steeling herself to descend the stone steps. But there, blocking her way, was John Roberts. "Didn't fancy the guided tour?" he sneered, bracing his arms against the walls. "Me neither. It's much more fun doing it on my own."

Marnie stared at him, suddenly, unaccountably terrified. "Nobody's stopping you from creeping around on your own, but you are *not* coming with me," she said fiercely. "Let me through, OK?"

John smirked and dropped his arms. "Nobody's stopping you," he said coolly.

Marnie went. Down...down...down into the murky depths of Tantallon Castle. She lit the way with a flashlight that she'd brought, knowing that there was hardly likely to be electric lighting. Hurrying past walls that glistened with moisture, she went on and on, further into the unknown. But before long, her echoing footsteps made her feel alone and afraid. The enormity of her task was beginning to terrify her. Terrible thoughts whirled around her mind. What if this wizard was really a bad guy? What if she was walking into a trap? Suddenly, Marnie realised that she needed company. And only the Shoebox Zoo would do. Quickly, she freed them from her backpack.

"The Inner Sanctum is this way," Wolfgang said importantly, after sniffing the air.

There was a tinkling sound as Edwin rattled his armour. "Well, if you'd rather trust the vagaries of a copied map over the wisdom of somebody who actually lived here...well...mpppff." He dissolved angrily into a flurry of unintelligible huffs and puffs.

"I'm the Chosen One, right? So that means that I get to choose," said Marnie. She peered closely at the map and then grinned. "As a matter of fact, Mr Preening Parrot, Wolfgang is dead right."

Wolfgang smirked at Edwin – just as Marnie's flashlight went out.

"Oh no…" breathed Marnie. It was absolutely pitch black, not a glimmer of light anywhere.

"There used to be torchesss on the wallsss that led the way to the Inner Sssanctum," said Ailsa helpfully.

"That was nine hundred years ago," Wolfgang reminded her.

"What are we going to do?" Marnie wailed.

Bruno, the gentle bear, had the answer. "Trust to your heart, Marnie," he said. "If you *are* the Chosen One, then you're *meant* to find a way."

Marnie clenched her fists and closed her eyes. It had worked this morning, right? Why shouldn't it work again? She began to concentrate really hard, pouring all of her energy into her task. "What did they look like, these torches?" she muttered.

"They were made of gold and held in the handsss of giantsss," said Ailsa.

"More," said Marnie desperately. "Tell me more."

"They were emblazoned with the castle's coat of arms," added Edwin.

With a glorious *whoomph*, flaming torches magically burst into life along both sides of the tunnel.

In another part of Tantallon Castle, Laura was looking for Marnie. And she wasn't enjoying the search.

"Marnie…? Marnie…?" she called hesitantly, glancing back in the direction from which she'd come.

In the shadowy distance, there were two tiny lights, bobbing about in the darkness. The lights began to move closer – could she hear laughter too? Laura didn't stop to find out. She ran.

Hardly able to contain their glee, Stewart and Dougie sped after her.

"Great. What are we supposed to do now?" said Marnie. Great stone slabs stretched from one side of the tunnel to the other.

"An insubstantial vision, nonetheless," said Edwin. "We used to walk in and out on a regular basis. Child's play." Confidently, he flapped his wings, launched himself haphazardly into the air and fluttered – *smack!* – into the wall.

"Not so insubstantial now, huh, Eddie?" Marnie laughed as the little eagle slid down to the floor.

Once again, Bruno knew what to do. "If you could *imagine* the torches and they appeared," he said, "maybe you could *un*imagine the wall and it'll disappear, hmm?"

Marnie closed her eyes and concentrated once more. She could do it – she *had* to.

"Concccentrate harder!" urged Ailsa.

An ominous sound of cracking and splintering shattered the air. Then, slowly, magically, a crack appeared, running jaggedly from ceiling to floor. The crack grew wider and wider.

"Come on, quick!" said Marnie, through gritted

teeth. "I can't hold it for much longer. Get in there!" For once, the shoebox creatures did as they were told and scampered through the trembling gap.

"Quick, Marnie!" called Bruno from the other side. "The wall's closing again!"

Too drained to wonder how she'd ever have the strength to get back through the wall, Marnie stumbled after them. And not a second too soon. Behind her, there was an echoing bang as the wall closed again.

CHAPTER TEN

The INNER SANCTUM

Before them lay a solid, wooden door, hung with cobwebs so thick and old they looked like dirty lace. Marnie pushed the door and it swung slowly and creakily open. She looked around in wonder. She didn't know what she'd been expecting, but it hadn't been anything like this.

The stone chamber was overflowing with furniture – a four-poster bed swathed in velvet, a battered old armchair, benches, shelves groaning with books, wooden tables... And on every available surface lay gadgets, weights and measures. There was an array of glass containers too – from phials and test tubes to jars and curved bottles – all brimming with liquids of every imaginable colour. A welcoming fire crackled and spat below a wide chimney, and candles littered the room, every flame casting a flickering glow over the whole magical place.

"The Inner Sanctum…" Marnie breathed. She gazed around the room before walking cautiously down a short flight of well-worn stone steps. Up close, she could see that the room was dirty and uncared for.

"Hey, what does *that* do?" asked Marnie, pointing to an ornate gold mask resting on a stone table.

"Oh, it's the great wizard's…oh, er, pardon me… the great early scientist's device for seeing things," said Edwin, hopping onto a long, oak table cluttered with weird-looking equipment.

Ailsa flicked her tail. "The wearer can sssee great dissstancccess," she hissed. "Maybe even into the future or the passst…"

As Marnie touched the mask it whirred into life, light pouring from between every carved panel. Ignoring the anxious looks of her miniature audience, she heaved the mask over her head and saw a scene that made her blood boil. Her own bedroom!

"Someone's been spying on me!" Marnie spluttered indignantly. How dare he? How *dare* he!

Edwin and Bruno gasped with shock, but Ailsa wanted to know more. "What elssse can you sssee?" she asked.

Reluctantly, Marnie placed the mask on her head once more. And what she saw then made her skin prickle with disgust – a smoky, rubbery film that was stretched and distorted by the inhuman creature that writhed beneath. She clawed at the mask, desperate to get away from the revolting image in front of her eyes. At last, she dragged the mask from her head and thumped it down onto the stone table.

"What did you *see*?" asked Bruno anxiously.

Marnie was pale and trembling. "Don't ask," she said. "I never want to see it again."

Abruptly, Wolfgang gave a loud, menacing growl and Marnie felt an ice-cold shiver run through her body. He was here – she knew it.

She turned her head slowly and saw a shadowy figure dressed in heavy, scarlet robes. He drew back his hood and stared deep into Marnie's eyes. This, at last, was the great wizard. His expression was weary beyond belief, as if he had suffered long and hard for countless years. His face was so worn that his skin looked paper-thin. His brow was furrowed and his eyes were dark, piercing and unreadable.

"So, you found me at last," he said to Marnie, then whirled to face the cowering Shoebox Zoo. "No thanks to *these* wretches!"

"We are sorry, Master…" simpered Edwin.

Wolfgang sank down on his haunches. "Please don't punish us any more," he whimpered.

With a terrible ferocity, the man turned on Wolfgang. "Who gave you permission to speak, *traitor*?" he roared.

Marnie flinched at the venom in his voice. "Hey, they're just trying to apologise…" she protested, even though she was filled with apprehension. What was *with* this guy?

As swiftly as it had appeared, his anger melted away. He turned to Marnie and spoke gently. "Do you know who I am, child?"

With a start, Marnie recognised him. This was the man she'd met on her eleventh birthday – the man who had begun everything by encouraging her to take the Shoebox Zoo.

"You're just that crazy man from the junk shop… and the library," she said bravely. She braced herself for the outburst that she was sure would come.

Instead, the man pushed his hood away from his face and met her eyes. "I am the great Michael Scot," he said. "Alchemist to the Holy Roman Empire… translator of the ancients…man of science…man of logic." Now his voice grew louder and more powerful. "I'm a mover of mountains, a shaker of foundations, and *THREE TIMES* I have saved you and these *creatures* from disaster!"

This was too much for Marnie. She hadn't asked to be saved, had she? She hadn't asked for any of this! And who did this…this…wizard think he was anyway, boasting about achievements? "Well, you can add spy and bully to your list, the way you've spied on me and treated these little guys!" she shouted.

Once again, Michael Scot's anger vanished. "You really *are* the Chosen One," he murmured. "Come, child. Sit here." He pointed to an old, battered throne. Reluctantly, Marnie sat. "And you…rogues and vagabonds. Come closer and hold your peace," he added.

Edwin, Ailsa and Bruno moved closer to Marnie and the wizard. But Wolfgang slunk away, slipping out of sight.

"So, what have they told you?" asked Michael Scot, gesturing towards the animals.

Marnie sensed steely darkness behind the great wizard's smile and wondered how much she should tell him. She stalled for time. "Um, well...their information's kind of unreliable," she said. "They told me they lost this Book of yours–"

"They told you they *lost* it?" interrupted Michael Scot, as the creatures trembled with fear.

"Yeah, *lost*," said Marnie. Then she continued hesitantly – there seemed no other option, not if she wanted to avoid being turned into a frog, or whatever it was that wizards did. "And then you turned them into...into what they are now...and how I'm the Chosen One...and if I help them to get back this Book, then you'll turn them back into people and everything will be cool..."

"You make it all sound very simple, child," said the wizard wearily.

Now it was Marnie's turn to be cross. "Will you stop calling me *child*?" she said. "My name's Marnie, OK?"

"As you wish," replied Michael. Then he began to explain. "I believe that the Book itself has chosen you to find it. Why it has chosen you, from eleven hundred others, over hundreds of years, I have no idea. I didn't

write that. But I do believe that the Quest has become your destiny."

Marnie leaned forward in her seat. *Now* she was getting somewhere. "So you wrote the Book?" she asked eagerly.

"Yes, *I* wrote the book—" replied Michael impatiently.

"What's it called?"

The wizard sat down and solemnly faced Marnie. "In Latin, the book is called *Codex Arcana Nefasta* – The List of Unholy Mysteries. It's also known as *The Book of Forbidden Knowledge.*"

Marnie's ears pricked up. This was much too interesting to skim over. "Why 'forbidden'?" she asked.

Michael Scot took a deep breath. He seemed suddenly uncomfortable, as if what he described gave him pain. "The Book contains deep and dangerous magic," he said softly. "It's the sum of all my work on the mathemagical texts." His voice became deeper and more sinister. "You may find it, but on no account can you open it… For inside lie all the secrets to all the rules of alchemy."

"Sounds like a real page turner!" joked Marnie.

"*What exactly am I saying that you find so amusing?!*" roared the wizard. At his words, a howling wind whipped through the chamber, scattering papers, breaking bottles and flinging Marnie back into the throne. Then, just as suddenly as it had arisen, the wind died.

Marnie gulped. "Sorry…sir," she said.

★

The schoolboy leaned against the battlements, staring down at the waves that crashed far beneath. As a tiny howl reached his ears, he whirled round. His young face wore a knowing smile.

"Too weak to resist me, my little Wolfie?" said John Roberts – but his voice belonged to another. And, as he moved towards the blue and gold wolf, he became Toledo once more. "Now, what news of the girl-child?"

Wolfgang bared his teeth. "In return for news, I need some guarantees," he growled.

Fury burned in Toledo's eyes. "You…want guarantees…from me?" he said slowly, as if unable to believe his ears. He lunged at Wolfgang, but before he could grab the little creature, a brilliant flash of blue light arced between them. "You dare to challenge me?" roared Toledo, clutching his hand in agony.

Wolfgang still trembled from the electric shock. "You cannot touch the Book, can you?" he asked weakly. "Just as you cannot touch us. You need me as your cat's paws… unless you can charm the girl-child into delivering it to you herself." He paused, then continued in a wheedling voice. "If the girl-child is Michael's Chosen One, why shouldn't Wolfgang be *yours*…?"

Toledo rubbed his chin thoughtfully. "Why not, indeed, my little Wolfie… why not?" he murmured.

Marnie knitted her brows and stared at Michael Scot. "Let me get this straight," she began. "You want

me to go on some crazy wildgoose chase that you choose to call the Quest, in search of a Book that doesn't exactly sound like a bestseller, that's been lost for hundreds of years, that's too powerful for me to open anyway. And you don't even know where to start looking?"

The great wizard was silent.

"Er…in case you haven't noticed," said Marnie, "I'm just a kid. A kid who's not even from around here. A kid from the States who knows exactly *zip* about you and your history." Marnie had had enough of all this. She clambered down from the throne and grabbed her backpack.

"If she'd been the Chosen One," Michael Scot said suddenly, "your mother would have tried."

The heartless words stopped Marnie in her tracks. "My mom is dead," she whispered, tears prickling at her eyes. Then anger overtook the sadness she felt. "Look, I don't *know* you. I don't *believe* you. I don't believe *any* of this!" She turned towards the Shoebox Zoo. "Are you guys coming?"

Edwin, Bruno and Ailsa jumped into the backpack that Marnie held open. So where was Wolfgang…? But Marnie didn't have time to wait – she slung the backpack over her shoulder and marched towards the stairs, ignoring the wizard when he called her name. She'd listened to enough magical mumbo-jumbo – she was out of here, and nothing he could say or do would stop her.

Well, almost nothing.

Michael Scot flung out an impatient hand and, at once, Marnie's feet sank into the rock-solid steps as if they were made of wet cement. When she tried to move, she discovered that she was well and truly stuck. "Let me go!" Marnie shouted.

In a flash of light, the great wizard vanished, to reappear on the steps above Marnie. "Listen to me!" he said urgently. "The Quest is not just your creatures' only hope – it is the world's only hope. Lost, forgotten, unconstrained by morality, the destructive powers of the Book have grown over the centuries. They grow even faster now." His gaze softened. "Perhaps it is unfair that an eleven-year-old girl who knows 'zip' about history should be the one to change it, but who ever said that life was fair?"

Marnie stared at him, so many thoughts and questions crowding her mind that she didn't know what to say.

The wizard passed his palm in front of Marnie's face. At once, her eyes shut and she heard Michael's words as if in a dream: *"Tell no one about this – think only of the Quest. Let your heart decide…"*

Marnie opened her eyes and discovered that she was in a tunnel once more – and very much alone. She shivered. It was time to return to the daylight. With no flaming torches to lead her now, Marnie hurried through the darkness, along tunnels, up steps, round

corners – until she collided with the one person she least expected to meet.

"Laura?" she asked, squinting in the gloom.

"Marnie?" answered her friend. "Am I glad to see *you*!"

Together, they walked out of Tantallon Castle to face the wrath of Ms McKay.

As the two girls trudged sheepishly towards the coach, they passed John Roberts. He leaned close to Marnie. "Find who you were looking for?" he whispered.

Marnie didn't reply.

CHAPTER ELEVEN

EVIL WITHIN

Toledo carefully stretched a pink rubber glove over his long, elegant hand before reaching gingerly into a small wooden box.

There was a blinding flash and the Shapeshifter sprang backwards. "*Owwww!*" he bellowed, angrily ripping off the rubber glove and flexing his fingers.

Wolfgang crawled out of the box, howling in pain. "Hurts, doesn't it?" he said.

Before replying, Toledo took a number of deep breaths. "Wolfgang, my dear," he said, his voice as smooth as silk once more. "*Los Contrarios* grow – and the more they grow, the *hungrier* they become." He pointed towards the sturdy wooden case set with four metal domes that he'd brought with him to Edinburgh.

Curiously, Wolfgang walked towards the box. "Los Contrarios," he murmured. "Are they what I think they are?"

Toledo smiled. It was not a nice smile. "Oh, don't be afraid," he said. "My little creatures are no match for you, yet. But soon they will have the strength…just as I shall soon possess the power to overthrow the great Michael Scot!" Toledo took a deep, calming breath and then smiled sweetly at Wolfgang. "Now, back in the box," he said.

Wolfgang slunk nervously back into the wooden box.

Marnie and Laura stood in front of Mr Kasmani's desk, waiting for the headteacher to tell them exactly how they would be punished for their behaviour at Tantallon Castle. But it was Ms McKay, who stood behind the headteacher, that launched the attack.

"After all the fuss that Marnie made about choosing the trip to Tantallon Castle, you two girls broke all the rules as soon as we got there!" she said, frowning sternly over the top of her glasses. "Mr Kasmani and I are very disappointed."

"Very disappointed," repeated Mr Kasmani quietly, as if he were more nervous of Ms McKay than his pupils were.

"I'm sorry, Mr Kasmani," Marnie said. "I just went off exploring and Laura was just looking for me."

"I was worried she'd got lost," added Laura helpfully.

Ms McKay was having none of it. "No, that won't

do. Mr Kasmani and I know you, Laura Niven. And I bet *you* were the instigator."

Marnie leapt to her friend's defence. "No, that's not–"

"But–" began Laura.

"But nothing!" snapped Ms McKay. "You will both write five pages on the history of Tantallon Castle." She looked at the headteacher, who nodded meekly.

"*Tantallon?*" asked Marnie, hardly daring to believe her luck. "All right!"

Ms McKay, Mr Kasmani and Laura all looked at Marnie as if she'd announced that aliens had landed.

"I want it on my desk first thing tomorrow!" added Ms McKay sternly. "That'll be all."

That evening, Marnie sat with hands poised above the keyboard, staring at the computer screen. It had all seemed so easy in Mr Kasmani's office, yet it was already 7.00pm and she'd written hardly anything. And perhaps it hadn't been such a good idea to offer to write Laura's essay too…Out of the corner of her eye, she saw Bruno skate round the glass surface of her scanner, cheered on by Ailsa and Edwin.

"Guys, come on!" she said, trying not to giggle at their antics. "You're *supposed* to be telling me what Tantallon was like in the olden days."

Ailsa slithered across the desk. "Well, for a ssstart, we didn't have computersss then," she said.

"We had to do our sums with a chalk and a slate and a great big stick," said Bruno.

"What was the great big stick for?" asked Marnie.

"Er…to hit us with when we got our sums wrong," said the little bear, hanging his head.

"The only one who never got walloped was Wolfgang," Edwin said, rattling his wings in an annoyed manner.

Ailsa sighed. "He wasss alwaysss the favourite."

"I wonder where he is?" Marnie pondered. "And another thing… You know that guy — the one who was giving the guided tour? McTaggart? I had the strangest feeling that I *knew* him — even though I'm sure I've never seen him before." She noticed that the shoebox creatures were looking uneasy. "Does *he* have something to do with your stupid Book?" she asked.

"Erm—" said Bruno, then clamped his jaw shut when Ailsa dug him in the ribs with her tail.

Edwin butted in. "We do *need* the Book, remember?" he said to Marnie.

"If we're ever going to regain our human form, hmm?" added Ailsa.

"Sure…sorry Ailsa," Marnie said thoughtfully. "I just need some time to think about the Quest, OK? And right now, I have to finish this essay. Come on, guys — help me out? I need to know about life in good old Tantallon Castle."

"Oh, very well…" said Edwin, clearing his throat and puffing out his chest importantly. "Ah, I remember it all as if it were yesterday. We shared a spacious chamber overlooking the sea—"

"We lived in the basement," said Bruno.

"Yes, yes, yes… But that was *later*," said Edwin, before carrying on with his story. "Oh, I well recall the bustle around the kitchens whenever a fresh stag was delivered. What excitement…"

Marnie grinned – this was exactly what she wanted to hear. Soon, her fingers were flying over the keyboard.

In the penthouse suite of the Balmoral Hotel, Juan Roberto Montoya de Toledo and his guest were about to enjoy their evening meal. Wolfgang daintily licked at perfect curls of butter, while the Shapeshifter relaxed with a glass of ruby-red wine.

"So, the great Michael has revealed all to his precious Chosen One," said Toledo thoughtfully. "The question is, dear boy, has the girl-child agreed to take on the Quest?"

Wolfgang swallowed a mouthful of cool, creamy butter. "She'll take some persuading. And we both know she must accept the challenge of her own free will." As he spoke, the little wolf's lip curled contemptuously.

"Then you must beguile her, use your sly charms…" Toledo paused to sip his wine. "If you do your work well, the Chosen One will lead me to the Book before Michael."

"Marnie McBride, a mere eleven-year-old girl – Michael Scot's Chosen One!" growled Wolfgang. He looked up at Toledo. "But remember, you have promised me that I shall be *your* Chosen One."

"I've made you no such promise… yet," snapped Toledo. "But, as a reward, you will be returned to human form – as will your fellow shoebox creatures. If that is what you desire for them, of course…?"

"I expect greater rewards in time," Wolfgang said slyly.

"Just do your job!" Toledo snapped.

"Copied," said Ms McKay the next morning. "Even the spelling mistakes are identical, aren't they, Marnie?"

"I guess so," Marnie mumbled guiltily.

But Laura wasn't prepared to give up just yet. "Isn't that an amazing coincidence, Miss?" she said hopefully. "It must be the way we're being taught…"

Ms McKay glared at Laura and continued. "So, how do you both know that the tapestries in the Douglas Tower's upper chamber were of the purest blue silk? Or that the kitchen cat was called Kirsty?" She paused dramatically and then looked straight at Marnie. "I think we all know that you copied your essay off Laura's – and she had no other source but her own colourful imagination."

"No, I didn't, miss!" said Marnie.

"You two girls clearly haven't learned your lesson,"

snapped Ms McKay. "Perhaps five pages of maths will wipe the smiles off your faces."

"But that's not fair!" squeaked Laura.

"Six!" said Ms McKay, peering over her glasses.

"But…"

"Do you really want to try for seven, Laura?" asked Ms McKay.

Laura scowled, but remained silent…until they reached the corridor. "You promised it was all *true!*" she accused Marnie.

"Well, *sure* it's all true," replied Marnie.

"Oh yeah? Where did you get it from, eh?" said Laura. When Marnie didn't reply, she went on. "You just made it all up!"

"No, I didn't. I promise, OK!" shouted Marnie. She couldn't believe how unfair Laura was being, after all her hard work. "You might have been smart enough to change a *few* of the words."

Laura sniffed haughtily and slung her bag over her shoulder. "Well, I'll be doing the six pages of maths without *your* help, thanks very much." And she stomped away.

Angry and disappointed, Marnie turned to go – only to find herself face-to-face with Stewart and Dougie, doing their very best to look fierce. And behind them stood John Roberts. As quick as she could, Marnie pasted a nonchalant expression onto her face – she didn't want them to think she was *scared*. She headed for the stairs.

"Get the bag," muttered John. When Stewart hesitated, he pointed a regal finger at Marnie. "I said – go and get it."

Marnie felt anger bubbling up inside her. Then, it was as if someone had flipped a switch in her brain. The world seemed different – darker, meaner, cruel even. Immense power like nothing she'd ever felt before flowed through her. She felt capable of *anything*.

Marnie turned to face her tormentors and then slowly, deliberately, she took the backpack from her shoulder, holding it out before her. "You want it?" she said in a low, menacing voice. "Come and get it."

Stewart edged forwards, then stared in astonishment as Marnie's feather pendant began to glow, pulsing with energy. Even John Roberts seemed wary, as if he knew that Marnie was the one in charge now.

Marnie concentrated her attention on the striplight suspended from the ceiling above them. It flickered… then *exploded*! The boys looked up in alarm as the light fitting swung down in a slow, heavy arc. It was heading for John Roberts. But, at the very last moment, he stepped aside and the light smacked Dougie instead. In what seemed like slow motion, Dougie tumbled to the bottom of the stairs, his nose gushing with blood.

Far away in Tantallon Castle, Michael Scot released his grip on the golden mask and fell to his knees in sudden agony. Through clenched teeth he groaned, "Marnie, you don't understand. When you misuse your powers, you slowly kill my own…"

In the corridor of Marchmont School, there was a dreadful silence. Marnie stumbled down the stairs and stared speechlessly at Dougie. Had *she* done this? Was she now no better than a common bully?

John Roberts smirked. "Help," he said carelessly. "Help. What an unfortunate accident."

At Tantallon, the great wizard struggled to stand, but could not. "There is someone else," he muttered. "I feel the power of another. *Who is it?*" He fumbled inside his cloak and pulled out a small, crystal bottle. Thirstily, he drank from it.

Marnie was gazing guiltily at Dougie. "It wouldn't have happened if you hadn't tried to steal the Shoebox Zoo," she said to John.

"Steal?" said John Roberts. He shook his head and smiled. "It was just for fun. Anyway, we were following you to let you know that we found your little wolf toy in Tantallon Castle."

"Can I have him back, please?" said Marnie, trying desperately to keep calm.

"Haven't got him on me," said John with a casual shrug. "But why don't you come to my birthday party? I'll give him back to you there." He whipped out a stylish invitation, decorated with Celtic symbols and signs.

Marnie was so confused she could hardly think straight. First he stood up for her, then he followed her, then he bullied her…and now he was inviting her to his birthday party? What was going on with John

Roberts? Slowly, she read the invitation.

"There's magic, games and crazy fun.
Come, join the party, if you can.
A riddle for the Chosen One:
What boy is father to the man?"

Tantallon Castle's most famous resident struggled to his feet and placed his hand on the golden mask once more. "Who *are* you, boy?" he demanded.

John looked beseechingly at Marnie. "You will come, won't you?" he asked.

"I–I think I'd better get some help," muttered Marnie and hurried away.

John Roberts turned to the ceiling and stared right into Michael Scot's eyes. He threw back his head and laughed manically. In horror, the great wizard flung himself away from the mask. "Toledo!" he cried.

CHAPTER TWELVE

A VERY STRANGE BIRTHDAY PARTY

Marnie sat forlornly at the desk in her bedroom, her maths textbook open. Ailsa and Bruno were perched on the calculator watching her when Dad suddenly strolled in, whistling casually. He was armed with a duster.

"What are you *doing*?" asked Marnie crossly.

"Oh, cleaning up," said Dad, looking anxiously at Marnie's desk. "Are your shoebox pals helping you with your homework?"

Marnie sighed. How old did a person have to be to get some privacy around here? "Do you want something, Dad?" she asked. "Because I'm kind of busy."

But Dad didn't go. In fact, he sat down on Marnie's bed instead. "I'm concerned, sweetheart," he said. "Mr Kasmani wants to see you tomorrow. He's worried about you…your work…your attitude. Do you know what he means?"

"No!" said Marnie quickly.

"And this boy, Dougie," Dad went on. "He had some kind of an accident. Do you know anything about that?"

Marnie didn't say a word. Even if she did tell Dad, how would she explain what had happened? He'd never believe her.

"I got a letter from your grandma and grandpa today," continued Dad. "They sent their love. And Grandma asked me: '*Is Marnie settling in at school? Is she coping?*'" He paused. "I don't know how to reply."

"Tell her I'm fine," said Marnie, her voice breaking.

"Are you sure?" asked Dad gently.

Marnie whirled round in her chair to face him. "Sure," she said bitterly. "I'm as fine as any kid could be when her mom's died, she's been dragged halfway across the world to a country where she doesn't know anyone and half the kids think she's a freak!" As she turned back to her work, tears trickled from her eyes. "Forget it, Dad," she muttered, rubbing at the first tears that had fallen since her mother had died.

"I was nowhere near Dougie when it happened," insisted Laura. "And neither was Marnie!" She and Marnie were standing in front of Mr Kasmani's desk once more.

Marnie remained silent. She couldn't have explained even if she'd wanted to, but she knew that the accident was her fault.

"Marnie *was* there," said Ms McKay. "And my guess is that *you* weren't far away."

Once again, Ms McKay was towering above Mr Kasmani from her vantage point behind his seat. But today, the headteacher was in charge. "Now, Ms McKay, I really don't see how Marnie could have tampered with the light fitting to cause Douglas's accident," he said reasonably. "Do you?"

Ms McKay frowned crossly.

"No," said Mr Kasmani. "Well, off you go, girls. But I'll ask you to write Dougie a letter of apology."

"Yes, Mr Kasmani," chorused Marnie and Laura. Eagerly, they escaped.

That night, the Shoebox Zoo watched anxiously as Marnie tossed and turned in her sleep.

Four hooded figures ran through long grass – one clutching the Book. Hot on their heels was another, clad in white. The four struggled up a rocky path to a cliff edge, high above the crashing waves. Fearfully, they watched their pursuer, the Book hidden behind them. Nearer and nearer came the figure in white. He slowly lifted his head, the white hood falling from his face to reveal…John Roberts.

Marnie started awake, her eyes wide with shock. Why hadn't she guessed before? It was so obvious – they had the same mannerisms, the same flamboyant gestures, even the same gleaming ring! "John Roberts is the hooded figure from my dream – Toledo the Shapeshifter!" she breathed.

"Why, the perfidious shapeshifting snake!" cried Edwin.

Marnie snatched the party invitation from her bedside table. "'*A riddle for the Chosen One: What boy is father to the man?*'" she read.

"Hey!" said Bruno. "Does this mean Toledo is John Roberts?"

Ailsa looked pityingly at the kindly bear. "Yesss," she hissed.

Her shock turning now to anger, Marnie screwed up the invitation. "Tomorrow, we get Wolfgang back," she said.

This was a party to beat all other birthday parties. The venue: one of Edinburgh's finest eateries. The guests: plentiful. The food: exquisite. The decorations: everywhere. Above the entrance hung a long, swooping banner. 'Happy Birthday, John Roberts', it said.

"Marnie! So glad you could make it," gushed the birthday boy. He was dressed in a spotlessly white suit.

"Sure. Just couldn't keep away," said Marnie, not even attempting to hide the loathing she felt.

"I have something for you, don't I?" John said, clicking his fingers imperiously at Dougie, who obligingly gave him an object wrapped in a white, silk handkerchief.

Marnie grabbed at the package, but John whisked it away, putting a brotherly arm round her shoulders instead. "You know, my dear, I'm terribly taken with your toys," he said. "In fact, when you and I are best friends – which we shall be – won't it be fun to play with them together?"

"In your dreams!" spat Marnie, shrugging off his arm. "You *stole* him from me – and I want him back." She lunged for the silken package. But, inside the handkerchief, instead of Wolfgang, there was a rusted, old pocket watch, its hands set to eleven o'clock. "Oh, real funny," she said bitterly. "Come on, where is he?"

John looked stunned, then furious. He grabbed the watch and clenched his fist, splinters of glass and metal showering between his fingers. "What have you done with Wolfgang, girl-child?" he spat out.

Marnie turned on him. "What have *I* done?" she shouted. "*You're* the wizard – not me!"

John Roberts' eyes blazed with a cold, inhuman anger. But, before he could speak, a new arrival burst into the room.

"Ladles and jelly spoons! Boys and girls!" announced a friendly clown. Or was it a clown? With a shiver, Marnie saw that it was McTaggart – the guide from Tantallon Castle – in another guise.

"Let's hear it for the Amazing…um…er…Amazo!" McTaggart said nervously.

To the astonishment of everyone, especially Marnie, there was a puff of smoke and a conjuror appeared – a conjuror that Marnie recognised as none other than the great Michael Scot. What were he and

McTaggart doing here? Did Michael think she needed saving again? Or were they here for some other reason? More importantly, Marnie thought, they should learn to get their facts straight. Didn't they know that eleven-year-olds were far too old for clowns and conjurors? Suddenly, she noticed that a furious John Roberts and his bemused guests had reluctantly gathered round to watch the show.

"Four pretty little creatures, without an enemy in the world," began Michael Scot, brandishing a silver tray on which lay all four of Marnie's precious creatures. Marnie started, and then relaxed when she saw that at least Wolfgang was safe.

"Without an enemy, that is," continued the conjuror, glancing meaningfully at Marnie, "except for *science*. The elements – earth, air, fire, water... No metal on earth can withstand the power of fire." He picked up Ailsa by her tail. "Even this beautiful snake will very shortly become nothing more than a puddle of molten liquid."

At this, Marnie jumped to her feet in horror. What was Michael doing now? He wouldn't destroy the Shoebox Zoo, would he...?

"Be calm, my dears. Be calm," the conjuror said to his audience, placing the creatures inside a silver ice bucket and lifting a jug filled with liquid. "Our friends would cry for water if they could but speak. But this is no ordinary water. This is Aqua Regia – the queen of acids..." He poured the liquid into the silver bucket, where it frothed and foamed spectacularly, gushing over the sides.

Marnie stared helplessly as the conjuror placed a silver tray on top of the ice bucket and then removed it with a flourish. Immediately, bright flames whooshed high into the air – and then vanished.

"Can we undo the mischief, I wonder?" asked the conjuror, laying a scarlet napkin over the bucket and waving his hand above it. Then he whipped away the napkin to reveal…a fluffy white rabbit. "Young lady," he said to Marnie, gently lifting the rabbit from the bucket. "Can you confirm for the boys and girls that the creatures have indeed vanished?"

Numb with shock, Marnie stumbled to her feet. She looked into the silver bucket. It was empty. He'd killed them. Michael Scot had killed her Shoebox Zoo right in front of her eyes. "Yes," she murmured sadly. And everyone – everyone except John Roberts, that is – applauded.

But the Amazing Amazo hadn't finished with Marnie yet. "They have gone," he whispered into her ear. "But if you are prepared to undertake a certain Quest, they will return. And if that is what you want, you know how to find me…"

Before Marnie could speak, the conjuror was addressing the audience again. "Thank you! And for my next experiment, I shall require a volunteer. Who shall it be…?"

Michael Scot prowled to and fro, stroking his beard

thoughtfully. Eventually, he came to a stop before John Roberts. "The birthday boy!" he exclaimed brightly.

John shook his head crossly and lashed out, then as the conjuror grabbed his hand, screamed in agony as brilliant sparks flew between them. "Or should I say *Juan Roberto Montoya de Toledo*?" asked Michael.

"Yes!" snarled John Roberts, as expressions of rage and shock chased across his face, briefly revealing the older, crueller features of the man he really was – Toledo.

Then, suddenly, there was a blinding flash. And when the smoke had cleared, both Michael Scot and John Roberts had gone.

"Anyone for jelly?" McTaggart asked the stunned party guests.

Marnie stared listlessly into her empty shoebox, surprised by how much she missed the four awkward creatures who had turned her world upside down. She lay down on her bed, still clutching the shoebox – and as her eyes closed, she was whirled once more into the dark and mysterious dream that tormented her nights.

His eyes cold and menacing, Toledo stared at the four figures that trembled on the cliff's edge. Then a truly dreadful thing happened. The Book slipped from its keeper's sweaty grasp and tumbled out of sight…

Marnie awoke with a start. A storm was raging – lightning flashed, thunder rolled and a fierce wind buffeted her curtains. She leapt from the bed and went to close the window. And outside, under the glow of a street lamp, stood McTaggart the clown, his make-up dribbling down a face that suddenly looked old and impossibly sad. Slowly, he shrugged at Marnie, squeaked his red nose and walked away.

CHAPTER THIRTEEN

A LITTLE KNOWLEDGE

"Well, this is very short notice," said Mr McBride irritably, as he attempted to hold the phone and struggle into his coat. "I'm sorry, Dr Robertson, but I don't know why we're even making this appointment."

"The school asked me to call you about Marnie, Mr McBride," replied the woman's voice. She had a terribly English accent. "They feel she'd benefit from a visit to the child psychologist. This is Dr Robertson at your service – PhD, BSc, M alch, BTh, FDS, Nec – but you can call me Joanna."

"Marnie is hardly crazy, Dr Robertson," he said.

"Of course she's not," said Dr Robertson smoothly. "But I understand that she recently suffered a bereavement – as you did yourself, of course – and perhaps that is the cause of her *problems* at school…"

Mr McBride seemed unconvinced. "I guess…" he muttered.

"Splendid, Mr McBride!" Dr Robertson sounded delighted. "Tomorrow morning at eleven, then. I look forward to it *hugely*."

But the voice came not from a child psychologist, not even from a woman. The person who spoke was a tall, slight man dressed in a white embroidered dressing gown, wearing dainty white slippers and lounging on an elegant recliner...a man who was better known as Toledo the Shapeshifter.

One snap of Toledo's fingers and McTaggart arrived with a cocktail glass filled with a pale, green liquid.

"Did you dispose of John Roberts?" asked Toledo, plucking an olive from his drink.

"It's like he never was, sir," answered McTaggart.

"And yet his wee spirit lives on," began Toledo, then his voice rose, changing into the unmistakeable tones of Marnie's new psychologist, "...in the bosom of Doctor Joanna Robertson." His shoulders shook as he began to laugh.

Marnie and Laura were leaning against the lockers, waiting for the school bell to ring. And Laura was staring at her friend in utter astonishment. "You want to go back to Tantallon?" she spluttered.

"I've got to find a way to unlock the Inner Sanctum," Marnie said.

"Why don't you use your superpowers to walk straight through the door?" sniggered Laura. "Or how about a secret password?"

"A password?" repeated Marnie, her brain beginning to whirr.

But Laura was more interested in the contents of her lunchbox. "Oh, yuk!" she said. "She put in digestive biscuits for my elevenses…" When Marnie looked blank, Laura explained. "You know, 'elevenses'? An eleven o'clock snack?"

"Elevenses!" exclaimed Marnie.

"Mums…who needs them?" grumbled Laura. Then she looked up in horror as Marnie leapt to her feet and bolted down the corridor. "Oh, Marnie – I'm sorry!" she shouted. "I didn't mean that about mums…"

But Marnie just ran, Laura's anxious cries echoing behind her. She hurtled home as if a whole crowd of Shapeshifters had been chasing her.

Back in her room, she faced the Tantallon website at last, ready to try out her theory. She selected the 'change password' option and braced herself.

"OK," she muttered. "I was born at eleven minutes past eleven o'clock on the eleventh day of the eleventh month, so…" She changed the password to $11 - 11 - 11 - 11$ and hit 'enter'.

Nothing happened.

Marnie let out the breath she'd subconsciously been holding. Well, that was it, then – she'd never get to Tantallon now. "Elevenses," she said grumpily. "Dumb idea anyway." She hauled her backpack onto her shoulder and slammed out of her warm, cosy bedroom into…Michael Scot's cold, dark and stone-clad Inner Sanctum!

"Wow!" she exclaimed, gazing in wonder.

"It's Marnie to the rescue!" shouted a little voice.

Marnie whirled round to see Bruno dancing about on a dusty tabletop. Ailsa and Edwin were with him, slithering and prancing for all they were worth. Only Wolfgang looked unimpressed. "There you are!" Marnie said. "Come on – let's get you out of here before that cranky old wizard gets back. *Sleep!*"

The cranky old wizard gave a hacking cough and Marnie turned to see him huddled in an armchair beside the fire. She was shocked to see that he looked weak and ill.

"Are you…OK?" she asked apprehensively.

Michael Scot pointed past Marnie and she scanned the cluttered table behind her.

"This?" she asked, picking up a tiny crystal bottle filled with syrupy green liquid. Michael nodded. "What is it? Wizard's cough cure?"

The wizard threw back his head and took a large gulp, while Marnie marched back to the Shoebox Zoo and carefully placed them in her backpack. "Serves you right for stealing my friends," she muttered crossly.

"As your power grows, so mine fades," said the great Michael Scot, in a voice barely above a whisper. It didn't look as if the weird syrup had made him feel much better.

"What power?" asked Marnie innocently.

"The power you misused on your school friend," he croaked. "Or was that an accident?"

Marnie blushed, suddenly feeling very uncomfortable indeed. "I don't know what you're talking about," she said.

"The power that serves the darkness within you," said Michael.

So now the great wizard was saying that she was evil? Marnie turned on him. "Look, I don't *want* this power – I don't *need* it," she shouted. "I never *asked* for it!"

Michael's dark eyes bored into hers. "You're the Chosen One," he said, his voice growing louder and harsher. "It is your destiny! Whether you want it or not, you *must* use it!"

"Must I? Why?" asked Marnie. Was this Quest really the world's only hope? She found it hard to believe that anything she did could possibly be that important. "Because you want to use me?" she demanded. "Like I told you before – no way!"

The wizard's voice was raw with emotion. "My strength is fading. Only the Book can restore it. And only you can find the Book... Don't you understand suffering, child?" He dealt the final blow. "I pity your poor dead mother."

For a moment, Marnie was numb. Then her eyes blazed as she felt pure fury rip through her. Michael Scot was thrown back into his chair by a blast of icy-cold wind.

Without warning, McTaggart sprang from the shadows of the Inner Sanctum and put a restraining hand on Marnie's shoulder. Angrily, she shrugged him off. "You didn't know her!" she stormed at Michael. "You're no great wizard!"

"It's time to go, Marnie," said McTaggart.

Marnie wondered briefly whose side he was on. Was he shielding the wizard from her fury, or was he protecting her instead?

"Go on, then – leave," said Michael bitterly. "Squander your gifts."

Gently, but firmly, McTaggart led Marnie to a nearby door and pushed her outside. Then he closed the door behind her with a bang and turned back to Michael. "So, the great and wise Michael Scot…" he said sternly. "So great that he can't see that the Chosen One is just a wee lassie. So wise that he uses this…this wee lassie's *grief* to turn her against him." His careworn face was filled with pity. "Nine hundred years we've been waiting for this. It is time. And yet my Master wastes it on cheap tricks and dishonourable words. That's not the great and wise man that I know."

The great wizard did not reply.

Marnie was standing on a pavement somewhere in Edinburgh. She stared angrily at the heavy front door from which she'd just been ejected, her breathing ragged and her fists clenched. Marnie didn't think she'd ever been so mad in her whole eleven years. How *dare*

Michael Scot speak to her in that way? Furiously, she stamped back up the steps and pounded the door-knocker. But no one came and – after a few moments – she set off back to school. There was music to be faced, so she might as well face it.

"I can assure you, this is a very serious matter, young lady." Mr Kasmani spoke in a low voice. "What would happen if we all just disappeared from school when we felt like it? There'd be chaos."

"Anarchy!" screeched Ms McKay from behind the headteacher's left shoulder. Marnie was beginning to think that she might actually be a ventriloquist and Mr Kasmani her dummy – he didn't seem to be able to operate without her at his side.

"I told you already," Marnie explained. "I just had to go home to pick up some stuff." She looked up at Dad for support, but he was listening intently to the headteacher's words.

Ms McKay had her own opinion. "It's those ridiculous toys, isn't it?" she said. "Let me take charge of them."

"No!" Marnie clutched her backpack tightly. Everything seemed to be taken from her – her friends, her school, her mother… They weren't going to take the Shoebox Zoo too.

"At least you're back safe and sound," said Mr Kasmani quickly. "Now, Marnie, off you go to class."

Dad gave Marnie an encouraging smile before she

headed for the door, but he hung back to speak to the headteacher. "Sorry about all this," he said in a low voice. "I'm sure the school's child psychologist will sort it out."

Mr Kasmani nodded vaguely, but Marnie had heard every word and she had plenty to say on the subject.

"Child psychologist?" she hissed at Dad outside the office. "You have *got* to be joking!"

the truth at last

A silvery crescent moon hung in the night sky. In her attic bedroom, Marnie was hard at work, trying to ignore the vote that was taking place.

"All those in favour, say 'aye'!" said Edwin.

"Aye!" said the Shoebox Zoo.

"Motion carried," said Edwin, flapping his wings with joy. "The Quest continues!"

If Marnie had worn glasses, she would have peered over them now. "I told him and I'll tell you – no way!"

"But you wouldn't have to do very much," Edwin said. "We could probably lead you straight to the Book."

"Last time we sssaw the Book, it wasss in the Inner Sssanctum," Ailsa added, her green eyes flashing. "Michael Ssscot wasss asssleep and we took a wee peek."

Bruno shook his head. "No, it was when Edwin dropped it over the cliff, when we thought Toledo was going to catch us," he said.

Marnie smiled grimly. "So you *stole* it, right?" she said.

"*Stole* it?" Edwin looked seriously shifty. "No, no, no… *Borrowed* it without permission. Sort of."

"Whoa!" said Marnie. "You guys are just a bunch of crooks. There's no way I'm going after stolen goods – and neither are you."

Wolfgang stepped closer. "How will you stop us?" he growled menacingly.

But Marnie wasn't frightened of a tiny wolf. "Easy," she said. "Back. To. *Sleep.*"

"Oh no!" said Edwin dramatically. "Don't send us back to sleep. Not now!"

Ailsa nudged the slightly hysterical eagle with her tail. "Edwin," she hissed.

"What?"

"We're not asssleep!"

Shivers ran down Marnie's spine. She'd said the right words, hadn't she? So why were they still awake? She didn't like this – not one bit. "In the name of the great Michael Scot, *back to sleep!*" she commanded.

There was a blinding flash and everyone shrank back from Marnie's computer screen. There glowed the face of the great wizard himself – the powerful, the weak, the kind, the selfish Michael Scot.

"*Has not one of you the sense to realise what's happening?*" he roared, glaring at the tiny creatures gathered in front of the screen. "*This is the beginning of your restoration! Having finally admitted to your crime,*"

123

you are one step closer to becoming real, live *human beings once again! All you need to complete the transformation is the Book…"*

By now, Marnie was fuming with rage. Would Michael Scot stop at nothing to force her into accepting this Quest? He was even trying to turn the Shoebox Zoo against her. It was time to take action. "Next time you want to contact me," she said, reaching for her mouse as a cowboy reaches for his gun, "send me an email." With a swift click, she closed the wizard down.

Toledo was relaxing in the bath, his eyes just flickering open as his semi-faithful servant tipped a bucket of ice into the seething, bubbling depths. "My thanks, McTaggart," he murmured. "And where were you this evening?"

"I had a few errands to run, your Hatefulness," said McTaggart nervously, scuttling away to scoop up more ice.

"Of course you did," sneered Toledo, rising from the icy vapour and leaning towards the curious wooden box that sat on a ledge beside the bath. The eeriest noises came from within – screeching, painful-sounding noises. Toledo lifted the lid to reveal four large spheres, each with a stretchy, rubbery skin. Dark, quivering shapes lurked inside – moving and moaning in the confines of their curved cells.

The Shapeshifter smiled indulgently. "So, my dears, the girl-child is growing stronger," he said. "But are we downhearted? No! For, as she grows more potent, so will she grow more disposed towards the Quest. And if she will not, then she will answer to you, my little darlings… She will answer to *Los Contrarios!*"

As he spoke, one of the spheres began to bulge and split and Toledo's smile grew broader. But, by the time McTaggart had returned, the lid was closed and the Shapeshifter was hidden beneath the smoky vapour once more.

A dark, hooded figure inscribed beautiful lettering onto parchment, when the nib broke and ebony ink trailed across the page… Toledo raced along a wide, flat beach towards the Book, which lay half-buried in sand. Suddenly, a hand reached for the Book — a hand that belonged neither to Toledo, nor Michael Scot…

Wolfgang watched the fitfully sleeping Marnie for a few minutes, before sneaking up to the window sill and hopping out onto the roof. Swiftly, silently, he padded towards the chimney, where he howled balefully at the moon.

A sinister, whispering voice curled all round the rooftop. "I do not come at the beck and call of wolf or man."

Zap! In a dazzling flash of light, Wolfgang was whisked from the roof to the top of the penthouse suite's grand piano. Toledo was running his fingers over the keys, playing a doleful, haunting melody. "You have news for me?" he asked darkly.

"I believe the girl can be persuaded to help us," growled Wolfgang, shaken from his unexpected journey. "When we find the Book, I will deliver it to your hand myself–"

"Fool!" screamed Toledo, banging the lid of the piano shut. "If you attempt such folly it will destroy you! Only by *her* hand can the Book be delivered to me – and only of her own free will." He pointed a bejewelled finger at the wolf.

In the blink of an eye, Wolfgang was transported back to the chimney top. He peered left and right cautiously, then spoke into the emptiness. "I will get my revenge. I can wait, as you must wait, Toledo. And you, Michael Scot…wait and see what I have planned for you when I become the *Master of the Book*." He threw back his head and howled, long and loud.

It was the next morning. Marnie slumped against the creased, leather armchair, hugging her shoebox to her. "Dad, do I really have to do this?" she groaned.

"Let's just give it a try, sweetheart," said Dad, patting her knee.

"Fine," snapped Marnie, glaring around the wood-panelled waiting room. Why was she even here? It wasn't as if some dumb child psychologist could solve her problems. This shrink was hardly likely to bring back her mom…or make friends for her…or go on the stupid Quest instead of Marnie, was she?

A heavy wooden door opened to reveal a tall,

good-looking woman wearing a pristine white suit. A beautiful ring glinted on her index finger. She peered over her glasses and gave a warm, welcoming smile. "Allow me to introduce myself," she said in a silky-smooth voice. "I'm Doctor Joanna Robertson. And you must be Mr McBride and...Marnie. Sorry to keep you."

The doctor looked kind and sympathetic. Against her will, Marnie found herself wanting to trust her.

"Now, I think Dad should wait outside while we have a chat, don't you, Marnie?"

As Dr Robertson led the way into her office, Marnie whispered into the shoebox. "Now you guys behave yourselves, OK?"

Left behind in the waiting room, Marnie's dad leafed through a magazine. He glanced up as two men clad in navy-blue overalls marched down the stairs. The scruffier of the two nodded politely at Mr McBride. "Good morning," he said.

"Morning," replied Dad.

McTaggart the cleaner got busy with his mop at once, swishing it over the chairs, round Mr McBride's feet and along the wooden banister above his head. He made such a fuss that Marnie's dad didn't notice that the other cleaner – the one with silver hair – was listening at the office door.

Inside, Marnie was finding a visit to the child psychologist not half as bad as she'd imagined. In fact,

Dr Robertson seemed more interested in the Shoe-box Zoo than she did in exploring Marnie's most secret thoughts. The psychologist wielded a huge magnifying glass and examined the carved figures, which stood like statues on her desk.

"What are they like, these little creatures?" she asked encouragingly. "Tell me about their personalities. Why not start with Edwin?"

Marnie waded in without a moment's thought. "Well, Edwin's kind of self-important," she said, ignoring the eagle's outraged expression.

Dr Robertson nodded seriously.

"I think that Ailsa's the real smart one," said Marnie. The little snake winked one emerald eye in delight. "Old Bruno, he's kind of slow, but he's real cute. And then there's Wolfgang...I don't know. I'm not really sure about him." She paused, watching as the wolf raised his lip in a silent snarl. "I don't know if I can trust what he says."

The psychologist's face was in shadow. "You hear him speak?" she asked slowly, before springing to her feet and tapping to and fro in her white high heels. Swiftly, she changed the subject. "Are you daunted by this room – and all these books?" Dr Robertson asked, pointing to the crammed bookcases lining the walls. "Do you like books?"

Marnie shrugged, the faintest suspicion beginning to creep into her mind. This woman asked the *weirdest* questions. "Some books, I guess."

"Good," said the psychologist. "There's one book I know would help with our problem. But you won't find it on any of my shelves, I'm afraid." She crouched down beside Marnie, running perfectly manicured fingers along the back of her chair. "It's a book that would help me to take away all the pain and anxiety you're suffering. But you and I would have to work together like…mother and daughter."

This was going too far. "I don't think so," said Marnie firmly, bristling at the suggestion. She couldn't shake the feeling that something wasn't quite right here.

"Oh, don't misunderstand me – I could never replace your mother," said Dr Robertson hurriedly. But together we might find the answers we're looking for – in that book. And that would be the end of all your troubles." Her voice became lower and more mesmerising. Despite her misgivings, Marnie found that it was increasingly easy to believe everything that she said.

"Trust me," said the woman in white.

Michael Scot pressed his ear against the door and frowned. Quickly, he turned and caught McTaggart's eye. "Get him out of here!" he mouthed urgently.

McTaggart did what he had to do. *Whoosh!* Mr McBride was drenched – clusters of soapy bubbles decorating his shoulders and water pooling round his feet.

"For goodness' sake!" gasped Marnie's dad after a stunned silence. "What are you playing at?"

"Oh, dearie me," said McTaggart. "I'm *so* sorry, sir! Come with me and I'll get you all cleaned up." He nudged and prodded Mr McBride along the corridor until they were out of sight.

Michael Scot watched them go, before clicking his fingers to summon his mighty staff.

"You bear a heavy burden, child," said Dr Robertson, waving her hand to and fro in front of Marnie's eyes. "Perhaps you'd like someone to share it with you?"

Marnie could no longer resist the psychologist's hypnotic words and her eyes were shutting. But through a fog of relaxation, she sensed that her pendant was beginning to pulse. She must wake up...she *had* to.

"My, that's a pretty silver feather. How it catches the light..." said the psychologist lightly, abruptly moving away from Marnie. "Was it a gift?"

"It – it was my mother's," murmured Marnie helplessly.

"Ah...I expect you miss her greatly," said Dr Robertson, her voice suddenly sounding very brittle and forced. She placed a firm hand on Marnie's shoulder. "Do you ever dream about her?"

"Sure," said Marnie, the insistent throbbing of her pendant forcing her eyelids open. "I – I miss her." She glanced warily sideways and was shocked to see dark hairs sprouting out of the back of the psychologist's hand. Even her fingers were hairy. Suddenly filled with dread, Marnie looked up and saw that Dr Joanna Robertson was now wearing a neatly trimmed goatee beard.

"Let's talk about your mother." The woman's voice had now dropped several octaves. "You're upset. You see, Marnie, grief is a very complex process. Sadness, anger, even guilt…"

Marnie leapt out of her chair and whirled to face – a man dressed in the psychologist's white jacket and skirt. Dr Robertson had vanished. "I know who you are," she exclaimed in horror. "You're Juan Roberto! You're Toledo the Shapeshifter and you're here to trick me!"

Toledo gripped the edge of the desk. "Your power grows apace, girl-child," he hissed. "But do you really think you can defy *me*?"

Marnie edged away, utterly terrified. But Toledo hadn't counted on a little, carved bear who might not be the brightest creature in the Shoebox Zoo, but was definitely the bravest. Bruno launched himself fiercely at the Shapeshifter's middle finger. He sank his needle-sharp teeth deep.

Marnie watched in amazement as Toledo lit up like a human firework. His smooth, dark hair unravelled and stood out from his head, while smoke poured from his mouth and sparks flew from his ears and fingers – even out of his nose. Screams of pain and rage echoed around the book-lined room, while

outside, two cleaners in navy-blue uniforms chuckled delightedly to themselves.

Toledo tottered for a moment on his high heels, before falling like a skittle at a bowling alley.

"Quick, into the shoebox!" cried Marnie. "Let's get out of here!"

"Well, at least you gave it a try, sweetheart," said Dad, smoothing Marnie's duvet. "Goodnight."

"Goodnight, Dad," said Marnie, smiling as she remembered how silly Toledo had looked. When the bedroom door had shut, she looked at the Shoebox Zoo. "So the Shapeshifter's still around, huh?" she said.

"Lucky his magic didn't work on you, Marnie," Bruno mumbled. He still looked a little ruffled, but very proud.

"I'm not so sure it was luck," said Marnie, touching her pendant. She was sure that not *all* of the magic in that office had come from Toledo.

"But it was funny, wasn't it?" asked Ailsa, flicking her tail. "Him dressed up and asking you all those silly questions."

Marnie smiled mischievously. "Tell me, how did it feel to be turning into little toy animals?" she said in an English accent. "Did you feel sadness, even guilt?"

Edwin, Ailsa and Bruno shuffled over the duvet towards her. But Wolfgang remained on the bedside table, watching with disdain.

"Wolfgang, tell me about your father," said Dr Marnie. "Did you love your father, child? Who was he?"

Without warning, Wolfgang's eyes blazed and he leapt towards Marnie, snapping angrily at her face. She shrank back in shock as Edwin and the others held the angry wolf out of her reach. It was only a bit of fun – so why had Wolfgang taken things so seriously?

CHAPTER FIFTEEN

MOTHER'S FOOTSTEPS

The white coach crunched to a halt and as soon as its doors had slid open, pupils began spilling out onto the gravel driveway. Before them stood Hopetoun House – an enormous country manor studded with row upon row of tall windows. Marnie had never seen anything like it.

"Hey, nice necklace," scoffed Stewart, butting into her thoughts. "Your boyfriend give it to you?"

Marnie decided that the best course of action was to ignore him. Stewart was quite obviously trying to occupy his empty hours now that his precious John Roberts had mysteriously left the school.

"Hey, I'm talking to you!" he said menacingly, pushing Marnie against the coach. "It lights up!" he exclaimed, as her silver feather began to glow. Stewart snatched at the pendant, but recoiled in anger and amazement when it sparked painfully in his hand.

With a satisfied smile, Marnie walked after Laura. But she wasn't smiling ten seconds later when a hefty shove slammed her onto the cold, stone floor at the entrance to Hopetoun House.

"Are you OK?" Laura asked, helping Marnie to her feet.

"Wonderful," replied Marnie. She winced as her knees began to sting.

"May I have your attention, please?" called Ms Arnott, the art teacher, who was supervising the school trip. Reluctantly, everyone gathered round. "As you know, we'll be participating in the museum's art competition today," the teacher said. "There's only one rule – your picture must depict something on display in the house." Her eyes scanned the crowd of pupils and her voice became hushed. "But watch out for the ghost of the famous artist – Monroe Henry. It's said that his bones are hidden somewhere in the house…"

Marnie could see Stewart glaring at her. Then he slowly drew a finger across his throat. Inwardly, Marnie scoffed. Did he *really* think she'd be scared of him? As if!

"Well, off you go!" said Ms Arnott cheerfully.

Marnie didn't need to be told twice, dashing along corridors, up stairs and round corner after corner, searching for somewhere she could be alone. Eventually, she reached a large room with blood-red walls.

But she should have made sure that no one followed her.

Stewart stepped after her into the room. "Arnott isn't here to save you this time," he said menacingly.

Instead of answering back, Marnie decided to take action. Compared to Toledo and Michael Scot, this bully was a nobody. She could deal with him easily. She gripped her pendant tightly and stared at a large, wooden casket on the other side of the room. Slowly and eerily, the lid creaked open.

"Did *you* do that?" said Stewart, his voice unsure.

Marnie smiled – her powers were working. Stewart backed away, scared now. Again, Marnie concentrated – this time on the wooden door, which slammed, blocking Stewart's escape route. He stumbled backwards, further and further away, until he was beside the casket. One more step and he fell against the wooden box, tumbling inside. "Stop it! This isn't funny!" screamed Stewart. "Wait – I'm sorry!" Then he turned to see the ancient skeleton that already occupied the wooden trap.

"Don't worry about him," said Marnie. "He's already dead." She focused her power on the skeleton and its skull pivoted to face Stewart.

He shrieked with fear. "Look, get me out of here, please–" But the lid fell shut, drowning out his words.

Marnie walked out of the room, feeling both elated and uneasy. Deep inside, she knew that what she'd done was wrong – that the power she had should be used for fair means, not foul. But she'd been forced to do it…hadn't she?

The great wizard who watched from afar wasn't so sure.

A beautiful, haunting melody curled down the spiral staircase of Hopetoun House, luring Marnie closer, urging her to climb. Helplessly, she went, searching for...what? At the top of the stairs, there was a closed door and soft, yellow light glowed beneath it. Marnie grasped the handle, twisted it and then pushed.

The door swung open to reveal...the cold, gloomy interior of Michael Scot's Inner Sanctum.

There, in front of a blazing fire, stood the great wizard himself. He held a polished violin under his chin, while drawing a long bow back and forth across the strings.

"A Stradivarius – given to me by the great man himself," said Michael in a low voice. He moved away from the violin, which continued playing in mid-air. Marnie was speechless.

"Beautiful. Priceless," he continued. "You see, Marnie, you can use power...or you can misuse it." The wizard snapped his fingers and the violin was silenced. Then it fell.

Quickly, Marnie dived to save the instrument, her fingers closing round the smooth, carved wood before it crashed to the ground. Reverently, she placed the violin on a nearby table and thoughts chased round her mind. She already knew that the way she'd treated Stewart was a step too far – even if he *had* deserved it.

Marnie vowed that next time she'd keep her temper.

Then a rough pile of thick paper caught her eye. On the top, there lay a painting of four unmistakeable creatures – one fierce, one friendly, one clever and one proud.

"She was a good painter, your mother," said the wizard quietly, as if making amends for his harsh words the last time they'd spoken.

Marnie hardly heard. "My mom *did* know the Shoebox Zoo," she murmured. "They *lied* to me!"

"No, they didn't lie," said Michael, "not about that. Your mother wasn't like you. She didn't have the power to wake them, which left a great sadness in her heart."

"Is that what killed her?" whispered Marnie.

"No. A disease killed her," he replied. "A disease so strong, not even *I* could cure her–" He began to cough uncontrollably and Marnie shuddered at how ill he sounded. She glanced quickly about the room and spotted a golden goblet on a nearby table. When she took it to the great wizard, he drank gratefully.

"Your mother never had the chance to fulfil her destiny," he continued. "And I will not stand by and watch the same thing happen to you."

Marnie shook her head in dismay. "But she *should* have!" she cried out. "She should've been the Chosen One. She would have completed the Quest and she would have brought the Shoebox Zoo back to their human form."

"Marnie, Marnie…" murmured Michael Scot, lifting a hand to her brow. "You can make it up to them." He gently touched her forehead and, unbidden, her eyes closed. When she opened them, Marnie was at the top of the spiral staircase once more.

"Hello?" she said, knocking at the door. Marnie noticed that the light that had glowed beneath was now extinguished. There was no reply.

Then, there was a feather-light touch on her shoulder. Marnie spun round, expecting to see Dr Joanna Robertson, John Roberts or – at the very least – Ms Arnott standing behind her.

"Laura!" Marnie gasped in relief.

"I've been looking everywhere for you," said Laura. "Wait till I tell you what happened!" She rushed on without waiting for a reply. "Stewart got locked in a wooden casket!"

"No way," said Marnie, her voice deadpan.

"Yeah, he's lost it," said Laura gleefully. "Tears, shaking like a leaf – everything!"

Together, they wandered through Hopetoun House, avoiding the room in which Stewart still protested loudly about his ghostly experience.

"What are you going to draw?" asked Laura, who had settled on an antique vase. "Arnott will kill you if you don't find something quick."

A Victorian clock standing nearby butted in with jangling chimes. And before Marnie checked out its antique face, she knew what time it would be. Eleven.

Subconsciously, she reached for her pendant. And as the eleventh chime rang out, her eyes closed.

A cloaked figure picked the Book from the sandy beach. His hood fell back to reveal his identity – McTaggart. Then he fled in terror. On the cliffs above stood a man in white. He looked down and saw the perfect imprint that the heavy Book had left upon the sand.

McTaggart ran on and on, looking back over his shoulder in fear. Before him was a gateway built from three enormous slabs of granite. Through the gateway could be seen a rolling landscape and, in the distance, a church spire.

As the vision faded, Marnie's eyes sprang open. She fumbled in her backpack for paper and pencils, plonked herself down on the wooden floor and began to draw.

"What's that?" said Laura, as the granite gateway and church spire began to take shape.

"I'm not too sure yet," muttered Marnie, her eyes fixed upon her work.

"You're supposed to be drawing something from the house," said Laura with a sigh. "Not from your head."

"This *is* from the house," said Marnie. She didn't know *how* she knew – she just *knew*. "I just haven't *found* it yet. Besides, it's a landscape and art teachers love landscapes, right?"

At that moment, the art teacher herself walked into the room. "Very nice, Laura," said Ms Arnott, peering over her shoulder. "You have an eye for detail." Laura glowed with pleasure.

"What's this?" the teacher asked Marnie.

"A drawing, Miss," said Marnie, without looking up.

"Yes, dear," said Ms Arnott patiently. "I can see that. It's quite lovely. But what's the subject?"

Marnie carefully coloured in the church spire before replying. "I'm not too sure."

The teacher's face fell. "Oh, Marnie..." she said. "There was one simple rule – draw anything in the whole museum. I'm afraid you can't enter this in the competition."

"But, Miss!" protested Marnie. *Why* was she always getting into trouble? Why did *nobody* understand?

Ms Arnott continued as if she hadn't spoken. "Unfortunately, this will affect your grade." She left the room, her face stern.

Laura looked sadly at Marnie, as if she thought this was Marnie's fault too. "Why couldn't you just pick something real to draw?" she said.

"This *is* real," said Marnie, her jaw set with determination. "And I'm going to find it." She shouldered her backpack and marched out of the room, leaving a totally nonplussed Laura behind her.

CHAPTER SIXTEEN

BLACK MAGIC, WHITE MAGIC

Marnie weaved in and out of the tall, white pillars that lined the half-moon-shaped courtyard. As she crunched over gravel, the sound of tinkling piano music reached her ears – it seemed to be coming from one of the nearby rooms.

The door was slightly ajar and when Marnie pushed, it opened easily. The music was louder now, accompanied by the trill of an unseen woman's laughter. There was the unmistakeable sound of footsteps, making their way across the highly polished wooden floorboards. Marnie followed the sounds with her eyes until… She breathed in sharply.

There stood Toledo.

"It's you!" she said in a low, accusing voice.

"*Tranquilo…*" calmed Toledo. "There's no need to be frightened."

Marnie simply turned and ran. Of course there was

a need to be frightened! This was the man who had actually changed his appearance – twice – to spy on her. "Get away from me!" she shouted, her voice rising in panic.

"I've been waiting for an opportunity to speak with you alone," the Shapeshifter said, laid-back as ever. Then his voice metamorphosed into another… "I tried to talk to you as one of your classmates," said John Roberts, "but you shut me out."

"No wonder you were such a creep," muttered Marnie.

Toledo's voice changed once more. "I tried again," said Dr Joanna Robertson. "And still you resisted…"

"You were a creep too!" replied Marnie. She spun round and made for the exit, running out into the cool, fresh air. Surely he wouldn't follow her into the open…

Toledo stepped from behind a white column. "*Tranquilo*," he said. "I'm here to *help* you. Before, I was merely attempting to reach out to you using whatever means were available." His tone was warm and friendly.

"You know, my teacher's going to be back any minute," Marnie said. She didn't like this at all – didn't like Toledo, didn't want to talk to him, didn't trust him.

"Then you'll want to find the subject of your drawing before she returns," said Toledo. "I know where it is, Marnie. I can *show* you."

Marnie stared in disbelief, suspicious of Toledo's motives, yet tempted by his offer. "Why would you want to help me?" she asked.

Toledo smiled warmly. "I'm on your side, believe me," he said. "I only want to help you find the Book."

"You want it for yourself, don't you?" asked Marnie. She couldn't believe Toledo, she *wouldn't*.

"There is black magic and there is white, hmm?" said Toledo, his white suit dazzling in the winter sun. "Michael Scot is the black magician. He seeks the Book for his own evil purposes."

"He said the same thing about you," Marnie said, turning to leave. She'd listened to enough nonsense for one day.

But Toledo would not give up. "Doesn't it bother you?" he asked in a wheedling voice. "Never having any privacy? Being spied on by a deranged old man? I'm the only one who can save you. I'm the only one you can trust."

At these last words, Marnie turned back. She already knew the identity of the only one she could trust. It was Marnie McBride. She clutched her feather, concentrated really hard and...

...found herself in a room lined with shelf upon shelf of books. In front of her was a tiny papier mâché model of a familiar scene, with a grey arch, rolling hills and a church with a gleaming spire. And beyond the model stood Toledo – with Marnie's matching drawing pinched between his fingertips.

"You see?" said Toledo. "You knew it was here. You saw it in your mind's eye – and I helped you find it."

"Er…no," said Marnie smugly. "*You* didn't bring me here. I did it myself."

Toledo could hardly hide his irritation. "Do you have any idea of what Michael Scot is capable?" he spluttered. "He can turn base-metal into gold, he can heal the sick and…" He paused dramatically. "He can bring the dead back from the grave."

In a flash, Marnie's feelings about Michael Scot darkened once more. "But if he could bring people back…?" she began tentatively.

"He could have brought your mother back," finished Toledo. "If he'd wanted to. But as soon as Michael learned that your mother was not the Chosen One, he had no use for her."

Instantly, Marnie's eyes filled with tears. "That's not true!" she said, her voice breaking. "He kept her painting!"

"Because he knew that her daughter would one day be the Chosen One," said Toledo triumphantly. "And the only way you would take up the Quest was for your poor, dead mother. *That's* why he let her die." He moved closer. "Michael Scot is not the only one with great power. How many times have you wished that everything would go back to the way it was before?"

Marnie's longing was so great, she found herself nodding.

"We can help each other," said Toledo. "All you have

to do is find the Book. Just trust your imagination…"

Marnie followed his eyes to the model and watched as a tiny figure dressed all in white appeared in the grey archway. Was it her? Could it be her? It *was*! It was *Mom*! Speechlessly, Marnie stared. And stared. Then her mother turned and walked away.

"I…" Marnie said to Toledo. But the room was empty.

Suddenly, Marnie noticed that her backpack had begun to bulge alarmingly and her fingers tightened round the straps. Then a tiny pompous voice began to squeak and she relaxed. "Can we get out now?" said Edwin crossly. "Have we missed *all* the excitement?"

Marnie opened the backpack and tipped the Shoebox Zoo onto the table. "I've changed my mind," she said.

"You'll help us?" said Bruno.

"My mom never got the chance, so I guess it's up to me," Marnie replied. She solemnly addressed the creatures. "Are you in?"

"We've been *in* for nine hundred years!" Edwin announced. "What we want is *out*!

Marnie couldn't help but smile. Then she found her eyes wandering to the mysterious Celtic shapes inscribed along the edge of the model. And before she had time to think, her pendant grew warm and she found herself reciting strange words:

"*Follow where the river flows,*
And she shall tell you all she knows.

Beneath an arrow to the sky,
Where great hearts never go to die."

"I didn't know that you could translate ancient Celtic runes…" said Edwin in wonderment.

"Neither did I," murmured Marnie, equally baffled.

Bruno scratched his bottom. "But what does it *mean*?" he asked.

"How should I know?" replied Marnie. "I haven't got a clue."

As if someone had flipped a switch, Ailsa's emerald eyes lit up. "That'sss *exxxactly* what it isss – a *clue*!"

Wolfgang said nothing, but quietly licked his paws.

Marnie leaned closer to the model to read the information printed on the museum's label. "Hey, it says that these runes were found in this archway in the Eildon Hills." She looked at the shoebox creatures with growing excitement. "Maybe the Book's still there…"

That evening, Dad knocked quietly at Marnie's door. "I just got a call from school," he said.

Marnie slumped down in her seat, feeling her excitement trickling away. Why was she always in so much trouble lately? Couldn't *anyone* give her a break and just let her get on with her search for the Book? Once she'd found it, she *knew* that everything would be all right.

"When were you going to tell me that you'd won

147

the art competition?" Dad asked, his face breaking into a huge smile.

"Oh yeah," said Marnie as relief rushed through her. Ms Arnott had changed her mind about entering Marnie's picture in the competition once she'd seen the papier mâché model. But she hadn't expected to win.

"Well, you must get the gene from your mother, because I can't even paint a wall," joked Dad. "She'd be proud of you. I know I am."

That night, as she snuggled beneath her duvet, Marnie felt neither scared nor anxious nor angry. She felt proud.

CHAPTER SEVENTEEN

UNDER STORMY SKIES

"Since when were you interested in anything as 'uncool' as camping?" asked Dad, flipping his indicator and then pulling out into the traffic. He looked by far the happiest Marnie had seen him in a long time.

"Since you brought me to this armpit?" replied Marnie. She felt in pretty good spirits herself, though – the Book was within her sights, she just knew it. And, hey, the prospect of a night under canvas wasn't totally unappealing. "I want to breathe some fresh air for a change," she added, with a grin.

But just minutes after they'd set off, Dad stopped the car at the side of the road. "Er, Dad...what are you doing?" asked Marnie.

"Picking up your friends," said Dad calmly. There on the pavement stood Laura and Dougie.

Marnie bit her lip with disappointment. How in

149

Michael Scot's name was she going to search for the Book if she had company? OK, she could trust Laura, but what about Dougie? He'd only just started hanging around with them. How did she know that he wouldn't run straight back to Stewart with tales of her 'poxy' Shoebox Zoo?

At that moment, the tattered old shoebox was sitting in the boot, squeezed in between a camping stove and a large backpack. And inside the shoebox, something very strange indeed was happening to Wolfgang. The wooden wolf was changing – becoming lighter and brighter until he burned as brilliantly as a light bulb, until… *Ping!* He vanished.

Edwin, Ailsa and Bruno stared at each other in astonishment.

"Poor little Wolfgang…that you should be the subject of my little experiment." An entirely unrepentant Toledo smiled at the tiny wolf, who growled crossly as sparks flew from his carved fur.

"What are you up to, Toledo?" said Wolfgang suspiciously. "Why have you brought me here?" They were in the back of the Shapeshifter's luxurious car. As usual, McTaggart was at the wheel.

"Flexing my muscle…testing my power," replied Toledo, sipping from an elegant champagne flute. "The Day of Reckoning approaches, when all that is rightfully mine will be returned and the name of Michael Scot will be ripped from the pages of history!"

Wolfgang swayed as the car swept round a corner, his paws clinging to the leather seat. "I assume you had another reason for dragging me here – other than demonstrating your powers…?" he sneered.

Toledo snapped his fingers and a stainless-steel cigarette lighter appeared in his hand. A flick of his wrist later and a tall flame leapt into the air. "You see how close your nose is to the flame?" he whispered to Wolfgang. That's how close the girl-child is to finding the Book. So if you value your face – indeed, your whole pathetic wooden frame – then you'll bring me the clue that she found at Hopetoun House."

Wolfgang snarled under his breath, but Toledo hadn't quite finished.

"Otherwise, when she finds the Book for me," he continued nastily, "I may forget all about returning you to human form…"

The little wolf flinched.

They'd found the perfect spot for camping – a small, grassy area that was level, sheltered and – best of all, from Marnie's point of view – in the heart of the Eildon Hills.

"Dougie, give me a hand," called Dad. He was clutching a handful of tent pegs, brandishing a rubber mallet and wearing a broad smile. "Right, last team to finish washes up after dinner, OK?"

The next twenty minutes were a whirl of frenzied activity, as the two teams battled for supremacy.

The girls' tent was a high-tech contraption, while Dad and Dougie were putting together an old-fashioned triangular tent.

"We're done!" announced Laura, hammering in her last tent peg.

"How did you do that so fast?" said Dad, admiring their handiwork.

Marnie shrugged happily. "I guess we're the experts," she replied and Laura nodded in agreement.

As the girls went to help the others, three tiny heads peered round the side of their tent. "Right, then," said Edwin. "Let's review our notes and instigate our search."

"Without Marnie?" asked Ailsa.

Edwin took a large, important breath. "Think of the glory of it," he said. "The first hand, nay, the first *wing* to touch the Book of Forbidden Knowledge in hundreds of years…"

"But what about Wolfgang?" Bruno said anxiously. "What if the Shapeshifter has him?"

"If the Shapeshifter does have him – and there's no evidence that that is the case – then there's not a lot we can do, is there?" replied Edwin, fluttering and skipping towards the zippered door of the tent.

Ailsa wasn't so sure. "We ssshouldn't let Marnie out of our sssight!" she hissed. "I'm ssstill not sssure I trussst her…"

"You don't trust *anyone*, Ailsa," mumbled Bruno, leaning back against a nearby guy rope.

Twang! A tent peg shot into the air and *twang* by *twang* it was followed by the rest. The super light-weight, supercool tent collapsed into a billowing heap on the ground.

Across the clearing, everyone watched with expressions ranging from shock to amusement. "Looks like you experts need a little more practice!" Dad chuckled.

Hours later, long after the sun had set, Marnie, Laura and Dougie were huddled round a tiny, crackling campfire, toasting marshmallows above the flames. Marnie realised that they really were totally alone. The only sounds were the occasional hoot of an owl and the whisper of wind rushing through nearby bushes. All around, the darkness threatened, stretching long shadowy fingers towards them...

"Boo!" said a deep voice.

Marnie whirled round in horror, fully expecting to see Toledo. But it was only Mr McBride. "Dad!" she shouted.

"Sorry, I didn't mean to scare you," said Dad guiltily. He held the extra blankets that he'd fetched from the car. "It is pretty spooky though, isn't it?"

If Marnie's dad had known that they were all being watched, he might have been less flippant.

"What do you think they're doing?" said Toledo.

"Toasting marshmallows, your Magnificentness," McTaggart said brightly.

"I meant the other two brats! They're not supposed to be here," hissed Toledo. "Let's see if we can't get rid of the gatecrashers…" He filled his lungs and then blew a cold mist through the campsite. A swift click of his fingers and strange new sounds crackled and crunched in the undergrowth. Thunder rumbled ominously in the distance.

"What was that?" asked Laura, her breath turning into tiny droplets in the suddenly chilly night air.

"You're not scared, are you?" said Dougie, his voice trembling slightly.

Laura shook her head bravely. "Me? No—"

An ear-splitting crack of thunder seemed to shake the ground itself. Then rain began to pour. Without a word – they couldn't have heard each other speak anyway – Mr McBride ducked into the smaller tent, while Marnie, Laura and Dougie scrambled towards the big one. The rain drummed mercilessly onto the thin fabric above them.

The storm seemed horribly close.

"What is wrong with these children?" demanded Toledo, a raindrop hanging precariously from the end of his thin, pointed nose.

McTaggart shivered. "Perhaps they don't want to get wet, sir?" he asked.

Toledo knelt down beside a rock and spoke to the miniature wolf that stood there. "The Book is in these hills, Wolfgang," he said. "I can *taste* it. Now, go in there and scare those brats away. The Chosen One has work to do."

"And how am I supposed to scare them?" asked Wolfgang.

The Shapeshifter threw his arms wide. "You're a wolf, aren't you? Snarl! Bare your fangs! Chew off an arm if you have to!"

A tall, hooded figure whispered, "Marnie, Marnie"...while McTaggart banged urgently on a huge, wooden door.

"Hide the Book – *hide* it!" mumbled Marnie, tossing and turning in her sleep.

McTaggart looked up as the door opened. Quickly, he made his way across an empty courtyard, before pounding on another door. It opened and McTaggart spoke quickly to the cloaked figure inside.

"Oh no! You gave the Book away!" Marnie moaned.

By now, Laura and Dougie had awoken and were watching her fearfully. They didn't see a tiny wolf crouching near the tent's entrance.

Toledo was becoming increasingly impatient. "I don't hear screaming," he hissed at McTaggart. "I don't see frightened children running for their lives!" He clicked his fingers – and the rain ceased abruptly.

McTaggart watched as Toledo shut his eyes and stretched his arms wide. "Get the Book... Must get the Book..." he chanted.

★

"Get the Book… Must get the Book…" But although Marnie's lips mouthed the words, the voice belonged to another.

Laura and Dougie stared at the sleeping Marnie, but then a fierce growl outside the tent made them turn their heads. There, silhouetted against the side of the tent was the huge shadow of a wolf! It threw back its head and howled.

"Wolf!" shrieked Laura.

Her cry woke Marnie, who joined in the screaming as soon as she saw the terrible shadow. Now, it was pawing the ground impatiently – increasingly blood-curdling sounds coming from its deadly jaws.

They'd heard and seen enough. Marnie, Laura and Dougie scrambled out of their sleeping bags, dragged open the zip and ran for it – straight across the clearing towards Dad's little tent.

"What's going on?" asked Dad, unzipping the tent opening. The girls shot past him without answering, but Mr McBride caught Dougie within the beam of his flashlight.

"Didn't you hear it?" wailed Dougie, his eyes wide with terror. "There's a *wolf*!" He too scuttled inside the tent.

"Wolves?" murmured Dad. "There haven't been wolves in Scotland for centuries…"

Swiftly, the wolf silhouette twisted and warped until it became that of Toledo – the Shapeshifter. He stood, methodically cracking each of his knuckles and his neck. Then he stepped into the abandoned tent and rifled greedily through Marnie's belongings. It didn't take him long to find what he was looking for – a crumpled piece of paper. He read the words that were scribbled there.

"*Follow where the river flows,*
And she shall tell you all she knows.
Beneath an arrow to the sky,
Where great hearts never go to die," he murmured, before slipping quietly out of the tent.

CHAPTER EIGHTEEN

WHERE THE RIVER FLOWS

Sausages and bacon sizzled and spat alongside each other in the tiny frying pan and delicious smells wafted through the campsite.

Dougie shook the pan gently. "When your dad invited me camping, I didn't think I'd be starring in *Night of the Werewolf*," he said, with an uneasy laugh.

"I didn't sleep at all," Laura said.

Marnie looked around the campsite – it all seemed so totally *normal* in the daylight. "I guess we just imagined it…" she said. But even as she spoke the words, Marnie knew that she didn't believe them.

"Hi, you lot!" said Dad cheerily. He was wearing waders and clutching an impressive amount of fishing tackle. "I'm just off to catch us our lunch. Make sure you don't go too far from the campsite… in case the *wolves* get you!" He grinned and strode away.

"So what are we going to do today?" asked Dougie, dishing up their breakfast.

Marnie waited a few seconds before replying – long enough to make sure that Dad was out of earshot. Then she put her plan into action. "Well, this is so lame…" she began, "but my dad's made up a scavenger hunt for us."

"What's that?" asked Dougie.

"It's like a treasure hunt," Marnie said. "There's a list of things we have to find. But my dad is a total brainiac, so there are a lot of stupid historical clues. First we have to find an arch – then we have to solve a riddle–"

"OK, we'll do it," Laura butted in. "But *first* you've got to tell us why you were freaking out in your sleep."

"What are you talking about?" said Marnie warily.

"*Hide the Book? Run for your lives?*" Laura said.

"*The Chosen One?*" added Dougie helpfully.

Marnie took a deep breath. Now her own dreams were betraying her… "Some people talk in their sleep," she said innocently. "So what?"

Laura looked totally unconvinced. "Look, I thought I was your *friend*," she said. "But you keep covering things up. I mean, all that stuff about hearing voices and seeing things that you were going to tell me about and never did… It's like you have this whole other *life* or something."

This was uncomfortably close to the truth.

"OK, you're onto me," said Marnie. "I'm a gorgeous, rich secret agent posing as an eleven-year-old loser… If I tell you any more, I'll have to kill you." She gave a hearty laugh, but Marnie could tell that she wasn't fooling anyone – least of all Laura.

It was quite a climb. By the time they reached the top of the hill, Marnie, Laura and Dougie were puffing like old-fashioned steam trains.

"How do we know we're meant to go this way?" groaned Dougie.

Marnie reached into her backpack, frowning quickly at Edwin, Ailsa and Bruno, who blinked up at her in the sudden daylight. "Because we're trying to find this arch," she replied, unrolling the picture she'd drawn at Hopetoun House.

"What, *that* arch?" asked Laura. "Well, maybe that *was* an arch…" She pointed to a heap of large granite stones at the bottom of a gentle slope. A river curved nearby.

Instantly, Dougie's tiredness was forgotten and he whooped with delight before bounding towards the stones. "We've followed where the river flows," he announced. "What's next?"

Marnie had memorised the verse. "'*Beneath an arrow to the sky, where great hearts never go to die*,'" she recited.

"It's just like your painting, kind of…" murmured Laura. Then, wordlessly, she and Dougie joined hands above the stones.

Marnie peered through the human arch and drew in a shaky breath as a ghostly spire appeared in the distance. Then the image faded. "Was there a church here once?" she asked.

"There still is," said Laura, letting go of Dougie's hand. "Melrose Abbey. It used to have a spire, hundreds of years ago."

"So what are we waiting for?" said Marnie. They were close – she knew it.

Dark grey clouds scudded across the sky above Melrose Abbey, while a cold wind whipped up the dry leaves into ever-changing heaps. The eerie sound of metal scraping against stony ground echoed around the graveyard.

McTaggart peered into a freshly dug grave. "Even if you do find the Book down there – which I doubt – you still can't touch it," said the chauffeur.

Toledo's head popped up above the ground. "No harm in making the girl's job a little easier, is there?" he said, before flinging the spade at McTaggart. "Finish this, will you?"

"'*Where great hearts never go to die…*'" murmured Laura, looking curiously at the crumbling arches of Melrose Abbey. "What's *that* supposed to mean?"

"What are we looking for anyway?" asked Dougie. "What's the prize?"

Marnie shrugged. What could she say – they were

searching for a book that she could never open? Yeah, right. "I guess we'll just know when we find it," she said. Then she had an idea. "Maybe we should split up… How about you guys go that way, I go this way and then we meet round the back of the abbey?"

Far away, in Tantallon Castle, someone watched as the boy and girl made their way past half-buried statues and headstones covered with moss, chatting happily about clues.

But Laura and Dougie stopped dead when they reached the open grave.

"This is way too creepy," whispered Laura, looking over the edge.

Dougie gasped in horror. "There's a skull and bones in there!"

"What else would you dig up in a graveyard?" asked a terribly English voice.

They froze and slowly turned to see a tall, thin man in a white suit. Beside him was a chauffeur clad in black. They made a sinister couple.

"Well, little boy?" said Toledo threateningly.

"Run!" shouted Dougie.

As soon as her friends had disappeared round the corner of the building, Marnie unzipped her backpack. "OK, shoeboxers – I want some help," she demanded, wondering momentarily where Wolfgang was. Was the little wolf totally incapable of staying put?

But even after Marnie had given them all the clues,

stressing the need for urgency, the three creatures looked blanker than an empty page. Marnie stared at them in utter frustration.

"Er…asleep for nine hundred years?" Edwin reminded her, hopping up and down crossly. "Hello? We can't be expected to remember *everything*!"

Ailsa slithered up a nearby headstone. "Doesss thisss have anything to do with it?" she hissed.

Hardly daring to hope, Marnie traced the inscription with her fingertip. "*Here lieth the heart of Michael Scot…*" she breathed.

At this, Bruno swayed as if he'd pass out. "No…" he wailed.

"It's just another wizard's trick, I'll be bound!" snapped Edwin, fluttering haphazardly over to see for himself.

Marnie noticed that more words had been chiselled along the top of the ancient stone. She brushed away the moss and grime that hid them, her fingers trembling with anticipation.

"*By the sign of the unicorn,*
When eleven is but one of a dozen,
There ye shall find it," she read.

The sound of pounding feet disturbed Marnie's whirling thoughts and she spun round to see Dougie and Laura racing towards her. Instantly, the Shoebox creatures froze.

"Marnie! Marnie!" shouted Laura.

"Hey, look!" said Marnie. "I found the next clue!"

"Forget clues!" Dougie cut in. "There are dead bodies lying around and two seriously weird guys following us!"

"What?" Marnie said faintly. She looked over Dougie's shoulder to see McTaggart running across the graveyard. Then Toledo materialised – much, much closer and heading right for them.

"Come on!" shouted Dougie.

Marnie didn't need to be told twice. She scooped up the Shoebox Zoo and stumbled hastily after her friends.

In the dungeon below Tantallon Castle, the great wizard spoke. "This has gone too far," he muttered.

And, in the shadow of the medieval abbey, a third figure joined Toledo and McTaggart.

"Where's the wretch that shares my blood?" growled Michael Scot. McTaggart removed his chauffeur's cap – and out Wolfgang leapt, landing neatly on a worn headstone.

Michael glanced dismissively at the little wolf before turning back to Toledo. "Your Day of Reckoning is closer than you think," he said ominously.

But Toledo shook his head. "It is your power that is waning, old man – not mine," he said. "It is your days that are numbered. My wit and cunning were always greater than yours. And with little Wolfie's help, I will *supplant* you!" In the blink of a metal eagle's eye, Toledo transformed himself into a wolf of purest snow white.

But Michael Scot didn't give the wolf time to pounce. He fired a bolt of magical light towards the Shapeshifter, turning him instantly into a tiny, pink-eyed albino rat.

McTaggart strolled towards the rat and picked him up gently, holding him towards the great wizard.

"Supplanted by a rat and a snivelling wooden wolf?" said Michael. "I don't think so."

Wolfgang shrank back fearfully as the great wizard plucked him into the air. Then he was hurled high into the sky, far, far away.

Marnie was sitting in the front passenger seat, dreamily watching the scenery whizz past, when Michael Scot's voice echoed in her mind: "*Marnie, at the signpost, put your hand out of the window…*"

Wordlessly, she obeyed. A tiny object flew through the air and landed – *thunk!* – on her outstretched palm. It was a wooden wolf, beautifully carved, painted delicately in blue and gold.

"What was that?" asked Dad, as she closed the window.

Marnie smiled happily. "Oh, I just needed some fresh air," she said, clutching the shoebox creature. She didn't know where Wolfgang had been, but he was back.

the sign of the unicorn

What did it all mean? Marnie stared at the science textbook, frantically trying to commit even the shortest formula to memory. She just couldn't do it. So how was she going to cope in tomorrow's exam?

"How can you even think of ssschool when we're ssso clossse to finding the Book?" hissed Ailsa, sliding across Marnie's desk.

Marnie ignored the interfering snake, but glanced up when a quiet *ping* signalled the arrival of an e-mail – it was from Laura.

Edwin hopped closer to the computer screen. "What's this?" he said, craning his neck to read. "'Too cool to be missed? A total freak fest?'"

Laura had emailed a link to a website too. "'Tonnes of people from all over come here for the festival,'" read Marnie. "'But the Pagan Mysteries is the night where the weirdest of the weird get together to party and hear wicked bands…'"

"There it isss!" Ailsa gazed at the festival logo – a dazzling, white unicorn – that was now glowing on Marnie's computer screen. "'*By the sssign of the unicorn, where eleven isss but one of a dozzzen, there ssshall ye find it!*'" she hissed, repeating the clue that she'd found on the headstone at Melrose Abbey.

"Ah! Ah! Ah!" squawked Edwin. "*The Book of Forbidden Knowledge* must be at the Pagan–"

That was it! Didn't they understand how much trouble she was in? Marnie slammed shut her textbook, narrowly missing the tips of Edwin's feathers. When she spoke to the miniature eagle, her voice shook. "I have failed every single science test this term. I have missed three labs and I have had two detentions. If I blow this exam, I am going to be kicked out! So, will you *please* just hush your beak?" She paused and then smiled. "In fact, you know what…?"

Marnie lifted a hand to her feather pendant, which had begun to throb with energy. Then she breathed out a blast of sparkling, glittering air that swirled around, picking up the creatures in its enchanted grasp. Edwin, Ailsa, Bruno and Wolfgang were whisked across the room and deposited safely into the shoebox.

"Hey, Edwin!" called Bruno cheerily. "You're flying at last!"

With one last puff, Marnie popped on the lid and – knowing how talented the shoeboxers were at

escaping – stacked some heavy textbooks on top.

She breathed a non-magical sigh of relief. *Now* she could get on with some work.

In the gleaming white penthouse suite, the spindly exercise wheel squeaked round and round on its endless journey.

"You'll wear yourself out," said McTaggart to the exhausted white rat.

"I can't help myself!" squeaked Toledo the rat crossly. "I told you to get rid of this blasted wheel! And get me *out* of this prison cell!"

McTaggart opened the door of Toledo's cage, slid a saucer of milk inside and then shut it firmly. "This cage is for your own good, your Extravagant Furriness," he said calmly. "It's not safe for you in the big, bad world right now."

The rat hopped off the spinning wheel and grasped the bars with its pink paws. "It's been more than eleven minutes," he protested. "More than eleven hours. Is it going to be eleven *days* that I'm trapped here?"

"Well, if you're lucky…" said McTaggart, with a knowing wink. "Michael Scot might have given you eleven *years*." He chortled to himself as he placed a large, white, silk cloth over the cage, hiding Toledo from sight.

Tomorrow had turned into today – the day of the science exam. Marnie desperately scanned her science textbook, but the words and diagrams instantly turned into indecipherable squiggles before her eyes.

"Did you get my e-mail?" said Laura, swivelling round in her seat. "You're coming, right? We're talking about the hottest bands on the planet!"

"Yeah, I'm sure my dad'll let me go," said Marnie, her voice heavy with sarcasm. "It's just a raunchy, all-night street party with thousands of total strangers." She sighed. After this exam, the only place she'd be allowed to go would be the library. To study.

Dougie leaned across the aisle. "Do you guys know as little about science as I do?" he said to Marnie and Laura.

"Hey, Dougie!" sneered Stewart from the back of the room. "One of the girls now, are you?"

"Wow, Stewart," said Marnie in a surprised voice. "You finally learned to talk in full sentences."

Laughter erupted all around, each snigger pushing Stewart further down in his seat. He seemed about to explode with anger.

Marnie turned back to her desk, silently jubilant.

"Marnie."

Even though she knew that the voice didn't belong to Ms McKay, Marnie glanced automatically at the front of the class. There, in an open doorway, stood Michael Scot. "Marnie, I need to speak with you," he said.

No one else was paying any attention to the great wizard, which told Marnie that she was the only one

who could see and hear him. Great – superb timing as usual. Immediately, Marnie stuck her fingers in her ears and clamped her eyes shut. But the voice persisted. "I know you don't trust me and I can't blame you. But you must *not* trust Toledo."

"Leave me alone!" she snapped. "I–" Abruptly, Marnie realised that even though no one could hear Michael, everyone could hear *her*. She had to act quickly if she were to avoid making a total fool of herself. "I mean…er…could I please go to the washroom, Miss?"

Ms McKay sighed and looked pointedly at the classroom clock. "Well, hurry up, Marnie. We start at ten on the dot."

As soon as Marnie left the room, Stewart sauntered casually towards the shelf near her desk. Making sure that no one was watching, he quickly slipped a folded piece of paper into Marnie's pencil case.

Marnie stormed into the girls' toilets to find the great wizard waiting for her. No surprise there, then – she might have known he'd pay no attention to the sign on the door. "Just. Leave. Me. Alone," she said slowly. "I'm looking for your stupid Book, OK? Quit bugging me!"

The wizard's knuckles whitened as he clutched his staff. "You're so close to achieving your goal," he said urgently. "But the closer you get, the more danger there is for you and your little friends."

"Yeah, thanks for the pep talk," said Marnie rudely. She turned to go, but Michael had other ideas. A blinding light sizzled round the edge of the door and, in seconds, it was magically sealed.

"Big deal," Marnie said. It didn't sound as if the wizard had any new nuggets of information to share with her – and she had a science exam to sit. With a defiant glint in her eye, she touched her pendant, summoned all the power inside her and...

...Marnie found herself back in the classroom, behind her desk. Thankfully, no one seemed to have noticed her dramatic entrance.

"Now, this may be a mock exam," said Ms McKay, efficiently dishing out exam papers to the left and right, "but it's still an exam. If I catch anyone's eyes roaming, then I promise you, the head attached to those eyes will roll. And for *some* of you," at this, she stared right at Marnie, "this exam will determine whether or not you have a *future* at this school."

Marnie gulped.

"You may turn your papers over," Ms McKay said sternly.

Marnie gulped again. The exam paper was as scary as she'd imagined. No, scratch that – *more* scary. She propped her chin in her hands and stared and stared and stared... Then, right in front of her eyes, Marnie's pencil began to scribble – first her name, then the date and then the answer to the very first exam question.

"I told you I could help," whispered Michael Scot.

And soon, the pencil had worked its way through nearly the entire exam paper.

"Five minutes, everybody," boomed Ms McKay's voice, her steps moving closer and closer to Marnie's desk.

Marnie panicked and grabbed the dancing pencil. Crunch! The lead broke, scattering black powder across the page. Marnie reached into her pencil case – she had just enough time to sharpen her pencil and attempt to answer the last question before the time was up. Her fingers brushed against a piece of paper that had been folded many times. Curiously, she opened it to reveal a list of scientific gobbledegook. She frowned closely at the paper, thoroughly baffled. She didn't know what it was or why it was in her pencil case. But she was about to find out.

"Come with me!" thundered Ms McKay. She snatched the piece of paper out of Marnie's hand and dragged her out of the class.

Stewart watched them go. He was smiling.

the night of the pagan mysteries

It had taken a considerable team effort, but by balancing Ailsa on Bruno's shoulders and using her tail to lever off the lid, the shoebox gang had escaped their cardboard prison. And they now knew that the kettle, the mustard pot, the toaster and the fruit bowl were positively, definitely unicorn-free. So it was time to ransack the study.

"Look at this!" roared Wolfgang, standing regally on top of a pile of photo albums. He was beside a photo of Marnie and her mother with their arms round each other, wearing identical smiles. Edwin, Ailsa and Bruno sighed in unison.

"Not *that* photo, you buffoons!" said Wolfgang despairingly. "*This* one!" He pointed a slightly singed paw to another photo. It showed Marnie's dad proudly shaking hands with his new boss outside the University Library.

"Yesss, very niccce," said Ailsa. "Ssso?"

Wolfgang smiled slyly. "The answer to a riddle?" he said. "The fulfilment of the Quest…?"

Now they saw it. Above the library door, there was an engraving of a prancing unicorn.

"'*Where eleven is but one of a dozen,*'" murmured Wolfgang, half to himself. "'*There shall ye find it–*'"

The front door slammed.

"Marnie?" called Dad.

The Shoebox Zoo looked at each other in horror, before revving up into full-scale panic and then – when it became clear that Marnie's dad was moving closer, not further away – freezing where they stood.

The door swung open. "What are you lot doing in here?" asked Dad curiously. He picked the figures up one by one and carried them back to Marnie's room, where he laid them gently in the shoebox. "I wish you *were* alive," he said thoughtfully. "Maybe you could tell me what's happening to Marnie…"

Just then, Marnie herself arrived back from school – and she wasn't pleased to see that her privacy had been invaded. "*What* are you doing in my room?" she demanded.

"Oh, er…" Dad changed the subject. "How did the exam go?"

Marnie couldn't be bothered with anything but the truth. He'd find out soon enough anyway. "How about…caught cheating, then thrown out of class? Oh, and lectured by Mr Kasmani." Her shoulders slumped.

"Cheating?" exclaimed Dad. He looked absolutely stunned.

"Ms McKay found a cheat sheet in my pencil case," said Marnie. "She thought it belonged to me."

"Did it?" Dad asked quietly.

"Great," said Marnie, flopping disconsolately down on the bed. "So now my own *father* thinks I'm a cheat."

"I'm not saying that," said Dad hurriedly. I'm just trying to find out what happened. Marnie, if you didn't cheat, there's nothing to worry about."

"I don't care!" Marnie was shouting now. "I just want things to be like they *used* to be. And how can they be when – when she…I miss her, Dad…I miss her so much!" At last, she gave in to great, noisy sobs, releasing pain and sadness with each and every tear.

Wordlessly, Dad knelt down and wrapped Marnie up in a huge hug.

"Sometimes, I – I see something on TV…" Once she'd started to explain, Marnie found she couldn't stop. "Or…or I read something or I hear a joke and I can't wait to tell her about it… but I – I– I ca – can't."

"You still can," said Dad softly, a tremor in his voice. "I talk to her every night. I tell her about the university, the leaking dishwasher and, sometimes, I ask her about *you*." He looked fondly at Marnie. "What do *I* know about eleven-year-old girls? I've never been one. Your mother – *she* was the one who always knew what to do. I'm lost half the time…"

"Half?" said Marnie. Somehow, she was suddenly starting to feel a whole lot better. "Try ninety percent."

"That's what she said." Dad chuckled, tickling Marnie under the chin. "Listen, I can't tell you that everything is going to be all right. But I do promise you – things *will* get better."

Marnie really wanted to believe him.

At Tantallon Castle, it was time for dinner. But Michael Scot wanted more than food. He reached his bony fingers towards the tiny crystal bottle…

"This might keep you alive," said McTaggart, whisking away the magic liquid, "but honest-to-goodness food will do body and soul a lot better." He placed a tray of steaming food in front of the weak and feeble wizard. When Michael Scot paid no attention, McTaggart waved a chicken leg towards him. The wizard's only response was a disgusted wrinkling of his nose.

"You'll freeze to death in here," McTaggart said in a matter-of-fact voice. The glowing embers in the grate were barely enough to take the chill off the room.

"Maybe I *want* to freeze to death," muttered Michael Scot. He looked up. "William," he began cautiously, as if he were unused to saying McTaggart's first name. "Do *you* think that the world would be a better place without me?"

"Feeling sorry for yourself, eh?" McTaggart's

voice was sharp, but his eyes were concerned. "Your ambition and your arrogance created that Book and you're going to have to be here to clean up this mess when it's finally found – now, *eat your greens!*"

As McTaggart moved away, Michael Scot snapped his fingers and the dwindling fire burst into life. Then he picked up his knife and fork.

Marnie glanced round the headteacher's office. Lately, she seemed to have spent more time here than at her own desk – it was hardly a claim to fame. Thank goodness her dad was with her, if only to shield her from Mr Kasmani's stern gaze.

"Now, Marnie's only been with us a short while, yet already she's chalked up…" – Mr Kasmani consulted Marnie's bulging file – "…late homework, lack of concentration, missed assignments, the incident with Dougie…and now this." He held up the note from Marnie's pencil case.

"It isn't even in her handwriting," said Mr McBride, frowning.

"Mr McBride," began Mr Kasmani calmly, "parents are often under the impression that their children are angels—"

Marnie's dad interrupted him crossly. "I'm not saying that. I am *assuring* you that she did not cheat. And, as for the rest of her file, well…I'll ask you to put yourself in Marnie's shoes – new school, new home, new country. That would be hard on any child, let

alone one who's just experienced a personal tragedy."

Mr Kasmani looked thoroughly uncomfortable, as if his underwear had suddenly been invaded by ants. "I'm sympathetic to Marnie's unique situation…" he said.

But Mr McBride hadn't finished. "If you were truly sympathetic," he stormed, "you wouldn't talk about Marnie as if she weren't sitting right in front of you. And, frankly, unless you and your staff start showing some real understanding and compassion for my daughter, we'll be looking for a new school." He got up to leave and Marnie sprang to her feet, trying to stifle the laughter that bubbled inside.

"Yes, well, thanks for coming in!" called Mr Kasmani in a slightly bewildered voice. "Always a pleasure…"

Outside the office, Marnie hugged her dad. She wondered briefly whether she should ask – and decided to go for it. "Er…does this mean that I can go to the Pagan Mysteries?" she said tentatively. "Please, Dad?"

Dad hugged her back. "On one condition," he said, his eyes twinkling. "I'll ask Laura's mother and if she says yes, I'll take both of you."

Marnie grinned up at him. Life suddenly seemed a whole lot brighter.

The Shoebox Zoo huddled together on Marnie's mantelpiece. A very important meeting was taking place.

"The vote, comrades, is a simple one," whispered Edwin. "The motion is as follows... Do we tell Marnie about the photograph? Or do we go to the place where eleven is but one of a dozen?"

"That'sss *two* motionsss," hissed Ailsa.

Edwin tutted. "Where have *you* been? The Hair-splitters' Convention?"

"Do we *tell* her?" repeated Wolfgang, taking charge of the proceedings. "All those in favour raise a paw, a wing...whatever." He glanced disparagingly at Ailsa.

There was a clanking, rustling and creaking as the creatures voted.

"Motion carried," announced Wolfgang, licking his lips.

It was a bitterly cold evening. No moon shone. But the city streets were alive with dizzying colour and light, set to the hypnotic rhythm of pounding drums. Wild dancers, musicians and street performers entertained the crowds that had flocked to the annual Pagan Mysteries festival.

After a couple of hours, Marnie's eyes were dazzled and her ears buzzing. She and Laura hurried through the throng, looking at the medieval costumes and painted faces of the performers all around.

"That was amazing," said Dad, leading them down a narrow alley. "But I think it's time to go, eh, girls?"

Laura seemed overawed by it all. "Maybe this wasn't the best idea," she said.

"What are you talking about?" replied Marnie. "This is cool!" She was having the *best* time. Now all she needed to do was find the unicorn… And, right then and there, she did.

A small procession lurched down the alley towards them – a group of cloaked figures carrying a banner showing a white, prancing unicorn. The procession moved swiftly, driving a wedge between the two girls and Marnie's dad. He reached out for them, but was borne away by the crowd.

Now Marnie and Laura were surrounded – squeezed, jostled and dragged further away from Dad, before the procession moved on, leaving them alone. Marnie heaved a sigh of relief, but immediately, panic surged through her again as she saw that the cloaked figures – who seemed to have become more menacing – were heading their way once again, the drumbeats growing louder and more mesmerising. In the other direction, there was a group of fire-eaters – their skin painted scarlet, their movements savage and frightening. As the two groups closed in, Marnie realised with horror that they were trapped. She had to act quickly. Marnie dragged Laura to the side of the alley, then leaned gratefully against the damp wall, momentarily closing her eyes…

A hooded figure placed the Book on a high stand. Then, she – her hand was too slender to belong to a man – picked up a quill and began to scratch Celtic runes onto an empty page.

Marnie snapped back to reality as, out of the darkness of the alley, there ran a brightly dressed harlequin wearing a beaked mask. Without a word, he grasped their wrists and pulled Laura and Marnie away from the fire-eaters, through the crowd of cloaked figures, past the unicorn banner and into a deserted alley – free from people and noise.

The harlequin bowed and removed his mask to reveal his identity. It was McTaggart. "Forgive me, but this is no place for two young ladies on their own," he said breathlessly, before speaking quietly to Marnie. "And that wasn't the unicorn that you sought."

Marnie had had too wild an evening for anything to surprise her now. She nodded quickly and accepted the piece of tattered parchment that McTaggart pushed into her hand as he muttered, "It's where eleven is but one of a dozen – hurry, before it's too late."

Ominous footsteps sounded through the alley – loud, stomping, urgent footsteps. Footsteps belonging to someone who was desperate to find Marnie and Laura. Footsteps belonging to her dad.

"There you are!" he said. "I've been looking for you everywhere – are you OK?"

Marnie nodded, relieved beyond words. As they walked back to the car, she lagged behind to open the parchment and read the words that were inscribed there…

"The text you seek is guarded by he who loves it best."

CHAPTER TWENTY-ONE

THE RIGHTFUL HEIR OF MICHAEL SCOT

It was Saturday morning. Edwin, Ailsa, Bruno and Wolfgang watched anxiously from the shoebox as Marnie muttered unintelligibly in her sleep, her arms flailing wildly.

"She's dreaming about us," said Wolfgang, his voice laden with doom. "Her dreams tell her *everything* – every secret we've tried to keep from her and more…" He glared at his fellow shoeboxers. "What are we waiting for? We *know* the Book is in the library – and it's our only chance to be human again!"

At this, mild-mannered Bruno burst into life. "No!" he boomed. "*She's* our only chance to be human again. It is written that only the Chosen One can find the Book."

But Wolfgang wouldn't back down. "And I say the only way we can make amends for our crime – though, heaven knows, we've paid enough of a debt already

– is to restore the Book to Michael ourselves. Why do we need this girl?"

"We *don't* need her," hissed Ailsa. "We've *never* needed her."

So, two were in favour of immediate action – one was against. Three heads swivelled to look at Edwin, who was unusually quiet.

"It's up to you," said Wolfgang. "Are you with us or against us?"

Edwin hesitated, expressions flying across his face. Finally, he nodded. "Er…for glory and for honour – the Shoebox Zoo shall find the Book!"

While Wolfgang snarled in triumph, Bruno hung his head in dismay. But the decision was made and he jumped out of the shoebox after Ailsa and Edwin and plodded glumly towards the door.

"I'll be right along!" called Wolfgang. As if he had all the time in the world, he slowly pushed the shoebox lid back into place.

"That wolf's up to no good, mark my words," grumbled Bruno as they left the room.

"Ssshhh! Sssomeone'sss coming!" whispered Ailsa.

Mr McBride's footsteps thudded down the hall. He stopped. The creatures breathed in sharply. Then he propped his briefcase against the wall and moved on. The creatures breathed out – and as they did so, they saw that the briefcase was open. With a flutter, a slither and a bound they were inside.

"Bye, darling!" shouted Marnie's dad. He shut his

briefcase with a *clunk* and swung it into the air. "I'll be back in a couple of hours – don't lie in bed *all* morning!"

"Bye, Dad…" groaned Marnie, snuffling her face deeper into the pillow. But then a tiny tapping noise made her sit bolt upright in bed.

"What do you think *you're* doing?" she demanded.

Wolfgang was sitting in front of her computer keyboard, using her e-mail!

A cheery *ding* announced that an email had reached Toledo's small, white laptop. Unfortunately, because he was still imprisoned inside the body of a white rat *and* a very sturdy cage on the other side of the penthouse suite, he couldn't read it.

"What does it say? What does it *say*?" he squeaked urgently.

McTaggart struggled to a sitting position on the leather sofa. His face was creased and his eyes were puffy. He looked *very* tired, as if he'd been working much too hard.

"Now, now, your Furry Extravagance," he said. "There's no use you trying to read while you're still a rodent – you'll not understand the human language. Just relax and get some sleep." He slid a large, white cloth over Toledo's cage and hurried over to the laptop to read the message for himself.

MASTER

MY FOOLHARDY FRIENDS HAVE DISCOVERED THE WHEREABOUTS OF THE BOOK. IT IS IN THE UNIVERSITY LIBRARY. THEY HAVE GONE THERE — ALONE. NOW IS YOUR CHANCE!

YOUR HUMBLE SERVANT

WOLFGANG

McTaggart went pale. Then he deleted the message.

Marnie pinched Wolfgang's wooden tail between her fingers and dangled him mercilessly above the candle flame. He drew back his charred paws.

"It was Laura!" the wolf cried. "I sent it to Laura!"

"Do you think I'm *dumb* or something?" said Marnie. "*Why* would you want to send an email to Laura?" She lowered him closer to the flame. "Now will you tell me?"

Wolfgang whimpered in terror. "All right! I sent it to the Shapeshifter – to Toledo. I – I – I had to report to him."

"Report what?" said Marnie.

"Nothing," said Wolfgang quickly. "There was nothing to report."

Marnie moved him towards the flame again. "You're lying!" she said.

Wolfgang was so near to the candle that a tiny flame was reflected in each of his eyes. "I just told him that

the others had escaped again," he said desperately. "That's all, I promise!"

"Why are you doing this?" asked Marnie. She was totally baffled by the wolf's behaviour – even though she'd never been as sure of him as she was of the others.

"He promised to restore the birthright that was denied to me," said Wolfgang. "When Toledo has the Book, I'll become the rightful heir of Michael Scot."

Marnie's first response was laughter. Her second was to put Wolfgang back on the desk – with outlandish ideas like this, he was obviously no threat to her or anyone else. "You?" she said. "The rightful heir of Michael Scot? I don't think so."

"Have you forgotten that I was human once?" asked Wolfgang in a low voice.

"What?" said Marnie, uncertainty creeping into her mind.

Wolfgang's next words made the hairs on the back of Marnie's neck stand up. "I am the son of Michael Scot."

"*H – he* did this to you?" spluttered Marnie. Then she hesitated. "Wait. You wouldn't be lying to me again, would you?"

"Ask him yourself."

"You know what?" said Marnie. "I think I will." She was bored of secrets and lies – she wanted to know the truth. Marnie wrapped her fingers round her feather pendant, closed her eyes and concentrated *hard*.

186

She felt the pendant begin to pulse as its magic flowed.

"Noooooo!" wailed Wolfgang.

But too late. In a flash of blinding light, both he and Marnie were whirled away...

...to Tantallon Castle, where a very frail Michael Scot stared into the embers of a dying fire. The Inner Sanctum was cold and dank.

"I think you've got some explaining to do!" stormed Marnie.

Michael was calm. "I knew the day would come when I would have to justify myself to an eleven-year-old—"

"He's your own son!" said Marnie. "Why did you do it?"

The great wizard paused before replying, as if gathering his strength for the ordeal ahead. "Wolfgang was a fine student," he said. "He would have made a worthy successor. And I told him to be patient, but he wouldn't wait. Again and again I told him about the terrible powers of the Book. I told him that when he was a man – *truly* a man – he would be ready."

"Yet even when I became a man, you denied me," said Wolfgang bitterly.

Michael continued as if the little wolf hadn't spoken. "All that remained was for him to turn the others against me. Soon, all my loyal students – even good-natured Bruno – showed dark ambition." He took a shaky breath. "I think you know what happened next."

She did know. "They stole the Book?"

The great wizard gave a brief nod. "And I cursed the traitors with a spell so terrible that it could only be undone by the Book itself."

"How could you *do* something like that?" asked Marnie with genuine curiosity.

"I was blinded by rage and thwarted ambition," said Michael, a growing anger filling his voice with power. "Wolfgang pleaded for mercy, but I wouldn't give it. I, the great wizard, the *architect* of the Book, who, in his vanity thought he could control its powers, had failed the final test – to control *himself*." His voice dropped to a whisper. "But not one minute has gone by since without my regretting that action."

Wolfgang approached his father slowly. "I have felt the same guilt, the same regret, the same torment…"

"Wolfgang, my son, I've missed you," said Michael, reaching out an unsteady hand towards the little wolf. "To see you as you once were – a young man in his prime…" he said wistfully. "But I fear that may never be – that the Book may never be found and this awful deed undone…"

As his voice trailed away, Marnie saw how grey and old the wizard truly was. She felt a stirring of sympathy and pulled a scratchy blanket over him.

"Thank you," murmured Michael.

Wolfgang crept closer and rubbed his head against the wizard's cheek. "Sleep well, father," he said.

"Goodnight, my son," replied Michael Scot.

"Hey, it's OK for you guys – you kissed and made up," said Marnie, who felt strangely left out. "I'm the one who's still got to go and find the Book. And I have no idea where it is."

Wolfgang took a deep breath and – stretching every part of his sturdy wooden body – stood tall and proud. "I, Wolfgang Scot, shall lead you to the Book," he roared.

where four
elevens meet

arnie's dad strolled into the University Library, put his briefcase – still laden with stowaways – on his desk and flipped open the clasp.

The moment his back was turned, Ailsa and Edwin slipped out of the briefcase and out of sight. Bruno wasn't so lucky. He was in mid-escape – half in and half out of the briefcase – when Mr McBride returned.

"What are you doing here?" asked Marnie's dad curiously. "Oh well," he said, gently placing Bruno on top of a pile of forms. "You make the perfect paperweight."

Four aisles away, Ailsa and Edwin were already on the trail of the Book. They scuttled between towering shelves, looking this way and that, their brows furrowed in concentration.

"Where eleven is but one of a dozen…" pondered Edwin.

Ailsa's narrow eyes flicked from side to side, taking in the rows of leather-bound spines. "There's more than a dozen books in here," she hissed.

Edwin clanked to a halt. "But...one, two, three, four..." He began to count, waving his good wing imperiously around the library.

Ailsa watched curiously.

"...five, six, seven, eight..." continued Edwin, his voice becoming squeakier and more excited by the number.

The silvery snake flicked her tongue to and fro with increasing impatience.

"...ten, eleven, twelve!" announced Edwin proudly. "Don't you see?"

"*What?*" hissed Ailsa crossly.

Suddenly, a great rumbling sound filled the air. Edwin and Ailsa only realised that danger was heading their way just before it hit them.

"Eeeeeeeek!" screeched Ailsa as they fled from the huge, roaring monster.

"Wooooooooh!" shrieked Edwin, his tail feathers perilously close to the beast's greedy mouth.

"Whoa!" shouted Mr McBride. "*Whoa!*"

With a click, McTaggart the cleaner silenced the monster's roar. "What can I do you for?" he asked, his voice loud in the sudden silence.

"Er...it's just that I'm going to take a break in ten minutes," Mr McBride said meekly. "Perhaps you could leave the vacuuming until then...?

McTaggart nodded obligingly. "No problemo. See me? I'm *invisible*." He wound the cord round the vacuum cleaner and pushed it round a corner, where he spoke sharply to the eagle and the snake that huddled on the shelf where they'd fled. "Now, you just keep yourselves out of mischief until your mistress gets here, right?"

Marnie's dad scratched his head and strolled back to his desk where he let out a groan. His temporary paperweight was nowhere to be seen. "Oh no… If I've lost that bear, she's going to kill me!" he said.

Right then, *she* was just outside the building.

"Look!" said the little blue wolf peeping out of Marnie's top pocket. "*By the sign of the unicorn!*"

Marnie looked. There, above the entrance, was an etching of the mythical animal itself. She grinned triumphantly at Wolfgang and hurried up the old, stone steps towards – who knew what?

Away from the hustle of the busy street, it was as if time had slowed. Marnie became aware of the hallowed atmosphere of the building and its vast emptiness. Her feet instinctively slowed. The Book was close – she could feel it.

When they reached the main library, Wolfgang leapt out of her pocket, threw back his head and gave a heartfelt howl. A moment later, Marnie heard a faint shout. She squinted up at the nearest bookcase and saw, perched on the very top shelf, the three missing shoebox creatures. Bruno seemed very out of breath.

"Yoohoo!" shouted Edwin.

"Hey, guys – what are you doing up there?" Marnie asked.

"Oh, a matter of little importance, I assure you," said Edwin smugly. "Simply solving the riddle."

"Really?" said Marnie, feeling more than a little sceptical.

"Oh yes…" replied Edwin, with a knowledgeable wink.

Ailsa hissed furiously.

"There's your dozen!" announced the little eagle. "The pillars!" It was true. Twelve tall pillars stretched upwards to support the great, domed ceiling of the University Library.

"So?" said Marnie, wishing for the millionth time that Edwin wasn't such a show-off.

"So," said Edwin patiently, "all we have to do is work out which pillar is number eleven – and there you have it!"

For once, Marnie had to admit that the eagle might be right. She scanned the room, taking in the tall pillars – identical in every way… Wait. One of them was different. "What was McTaggart's clue?" she asked the shoebox creatures.

"The text you ssseek isss guarded by he who lovesss it bessst," replied Ailsa helpfully.

Marnie hurried towards the nearest pillar and peered closely at the small painting that hung there. It showed

a Victorian scholar, deeply engrossed in a book. And the title of the painting was: *The Book Lover*.

Carefully, Marnie unhooked the painting and leaned it against the bottom of the pillar, where her tiny companions scurried to examine it, *oohing* and *aahing* over the cleverness of the clue.

In a fever of excitement, Marnie circled the column, tapping it and running her fingers over every surface. Then she felt along every join. Was it her imagination, or was one panel slightly raised? She scrabbled at the edge, her fingertips struggling to get a grip, when — *creak!* — the panel slowly began to come away from the column. No, not a panel — it was a door!

"Could the Book be here?" murmured Marnie. "Could it *really* be here?"

"Be careful, missstresss," said Ailsa.

Bruno had the final word. "Remember, Marnie," he said, "you're the Chosen One."

The time for wondering and wishing and hoping was past. Marnie stepped into the blackness.

As she crept forward, Marnie's eyes began to grow used to the darkness and she saw that she was in a tunnel — but not any old stone or brick tunnel. The curved walls rustled mysteriously, the surface flickering and shimmering with…paper! Open books, their pages fluttering and moving in an unseen breeze. Books above, below and all around. A tunnel of books.

"Marnie? *Marnie!*"

She was whisked away to the twilight world of the Book, where she'd followed its progress during so many dreams and visions.

The hooded woman bent over a desk, quill pen in hand. She opened the Book, then dipped the nib into jet-black ink, before drawing runes on a blank page. The woman looked up, her dark hood falling away from her face.

It was Marnie's mother.

"Even The Book of Forbidden Knowledge is not always what it seems," she said.

Marnie's mother took the Book and placed it inside a wooden barrel, which she carried to a tree in the courtyard.

Marnie took a hesitant step forward. Open books hung from the roof of the tunnel. With a gentle swish, they parted to reveal a brilliant light. She shaded her eyes, then watched in amazement as a hooded figure approached. Could it be…?

The hooded figure looked up and the familiar face that Marnie knew so well gazed back at her. "Marnie. Don't be afraid, my baby," she said in her beautiful, gentle voice.

"Mom…" Marnie breathed.

Marnie's mother beckoned her closer and, wordlessly, Marnie obeyed. But as she drew close, her mother melted away. And right where she'd stood, there was a small pile of books – with the prize that Marnie had sought for so long balanced on top, glowing as brightly as Marnie's pendant.

Marnie stretched out her fingers to touch the soft leather cover and the cold, metal clasps. She'd found it at last. The long-lost *Book of Forbidden Knowledge*.

Far away in Tantallon, Michael Scot woke from his slumbers with a start. "She has found it," he said.

"She has found it!" squeaked the white rat. The bell in the clock tower struck eleven times. As the last stroke faded away, the rat began to stretch and bulge alarmingly before growing and changing into... Toledo.

"She has found it," he repeated, his eyes full of envy and hate. He grasped the rat's cage – which was perched on him like an outlandish hat – and tore it from his head.

Marnie stepped out of the tunnel of books into daylight, clutching the Book. Stunned, saddened, confused, scared, delighted, amazed... It would have taken days for her to describe the feelings that flowed through her.

"She's found it!" cried Edwin. "She's found the Book!"

"Hurrah!" cried the entire Shoebox Zoo, in agreement for once.

Marnie grinned at them. She could hardly believe that she'd done it – she'd *really* done it! In a trance, she carried the Book to one of the reading tables, laid it down and gazed at its worn leather cover, the beautiful lettering, the golden clasp that held it shut. Without thinking, she reached for the clasp—

"Nooooo!" howled Wolfgang, leaping onto the table. "Remember what my father said! You *mustn't* open it!"

What had she been thinking? Of *course* she mustn't open it. Marnie nodded in agreement and put the Book into her backpack, zipping it shut.

"Marnie!" called her dad. He was marching swiftly across the library and wearing a very worried expression. "What are *you* doing here?"

"Er…I only just got here," said Marnie, thinking quickly. "I thought I'd give you a surprise."

"And everything's all right at home?" asked Dad. When Marnie nodded, he seemed relieved. "Well, it's great to see you. Look, I've done enough overtime for one day. Let's go home." In the time it took him to give Marnie a quick hug, all four of the shoeboxers had vaulted into his briefcase.

A few moments later, they made their way down the library steps.

"I – I've got a confession to make, Marnie," said Dad anxiously. "I found one of your toys in my case – the bear. And, well, I – I don't know what happened, but, well, I've mislaid him. And I'm really sorry–"

Marnie stopped him before he could apologise any more. "Don't worry, Dad," she said brightly. "He'll turn up, you'll see!"

Arm in arm, they walked home.

LOS CONTRARIOS

Marnie's fingers tapped frantically at the computer keys. 11 – 11 – 11 – 11. But no matter how many times she entered the password into the Tantallon Castle website, it bounced the same message back to her:

Your password is incorrect. Please try again.

"Why won't it work?" groaned Marnie. "Stop wasting time! I've got to get the Book back to Michael."

The Book of Forbidden Knowledge sat on the dresser in the corner of Marnie's room. Standing round it were four pocket-sized sentries – each one keen to become human again as quickly as possible. Right now, an argument was in full swing.

"Why ssshould ssshe have sssuch a problem with it now?" hissed Ailsa.

"No passkey," said Bruno.

"Pass*word*, Bruno," said Edwin, sighing dramatically.

"Whatever…" sighed Wolfgang impatiently. "Marnie can't get into the Inner Sanctum. So *we* must help her."

Edwin whirled to face the wolf. "And why, pray, are *you* so co-operative all of a sudden?" he asked.

"Didn't you know?" said Ailsa. "He'sss a reformed character."

Wolfgang's slyness and cunning seemed to have dropped from him, like an ill-fitting disguise. "You have no earthly reason to trust me – save one," he said. "After nine hundred years, I think that – at last – my father does."

Toledo was back to his cool, calm and perfectly-attired self. He sat cross-legged on the velvety-smooth carpet of the penthouse suite – his eyes closed.

"Which creature shall it be, my dainties?" he asked playfully. "The deceitful wolf? The untrusting snake? The woolly-minded bear…?" He paused, a sly smile spreading across his face. "No, the pompous eagle will suit us best."

In Marnie's room, the debate continued. But Edwin had suddenly found it very difficult to maintain his legendary level of pomposity. A voice was invading his thoughts – and it wasn't his own.

"Open it," said the voice. "Open the Book." The

words were soft and seductive. Edwin was powerless to resist. He moved closer to the Book.

"The first hand, nay the first *wing* to touch *The Book of Forbidden Knowledge* in nine hundred years," continued the voice. "What glory, what honour... What power!"

Edwin's wing hovered dangerously near the cover.

"*Open the Book!*" commanded the voice.

So Edwin did.

In an instant, Marnie knew that something was wrong. She spun round to see dazzling blue light spilling from the Book. "Nooooo!" she shouted, throwing herself across the room and slamming her hand down on the cover.

But she was too late. A blue-black, inky film drifted through the room, its greedy fingers reaching far and wide.

"What have you *done*?" demanded Marnie.

Edwin blinked and shook himself. His eyes flicked round his horrified audience. Then he screamed.

Outside, the bright sky had grown ominously dark. Inky streaks stretched over the Edinburgh skyline, floating over roofs and down chimneys...creeping sneakily into open windows and falling into chimney-pots. The dark shadows seemed to be slowly engulfing the whole city.

While McTaggart shivered as the feathery darkness touched his body, Toledo seemed to grow stronger, his suit glowing brighter and whiter. He smiled, striding across the room to his mysterious wooden box. Curious squelching sounds were now coming from inside.

"*Los Contrarios*," said Toledo in a sugary voice. "My pups! My cherubs! My dainties…" He opened the box to see the spheres crack open, spilling their ghastly contents. Four terrible creatures clambered out of the box. All were so dark that they actually seemed to absorb light. Except for their eyes – these were pinpricks of pure, dazzling evil.

There was a bear, a snake, an eagle and a wolf.

Toledo's hand reached towards them, quivering with emotion. "This is your moment, my little chitterlings – a moment for which I have waited these nine hundred years," he breathed. "The old fool Scot may have his hapless Shoebox Zoo, but I have *Los Contrarios*!" His voice reached a crescendo of excitement and he laughed wickedly. "McTaggart – make ready the car!"

The storm arrived out of nowhere, instantly transforming the sky into a maelstrom of wild energy. Thunder boomed, while lightning ripped the heavens apart and a freak wind whirled all around.

Then the lights went out.

"Oh, great," said Marnie, scrabbling about for her flashlight.

"Who knows what damage you've done, Edwin." Bruno's voice was full of despair.

"But I didn't *mean* to," whined Edwin. "I just heard this voice in my head."

"Relax, guys," Marnie said, her fingers closing round the flashlight at last. "It's just a power blackout from the storm." She pressed a button and swung a beam of soft light around the dark room.

Wolfgang blinked in the sudden brightness. "You think this is an ordinary storm?" he said miserably.

"What do you mean?" asked Marnie, bracing herself for the reply.

"*Los Contrarios!*"

"Los what?" Marnie frowned. Was Wolfgang speaking in code?

A shamefaced Edwin had the answer. "It means 'the opposites'," he mumbled from the safety of Marnie's pencil pot.

"One of Toledo's scientific experiments," explained Wolfgang. "He created them to seek us out and destroy us. He showed them to me, but they had not yet hatched…"

Marnie felt a cold shiver run through her, swiftly chased by a hot anger. Why couldn't anyone be straight with her? How could she ever hope to win if she didn't have all the facts? "And how long have you known about these…*los whatever-they're-called*?" she demanded.

Ailsa wriggled closer to Marnie. "Toledo told usss of them long ago," she whispered. "But we thought they were jussst a threat."

"Great," said Marnie sarcastically. "And he could be here any minute. So, if we didn't need to get the Book back to Michael before, we sure do now!" And if the password didn't work, she'd have to find another way to get in touch with the great wizard…

Suddenly, she knew how. Marnie grabbed her feather pendant, closed her eyes and concentrated hard. "Michael…" she murmured, using the power within her to blast the word across the rooftops of the smothered city, over the darkened countryside and finally through the walls of Tantallon – right to the Inner Sanctum. Nothing happened. "Michael?" she repeated, more anxiously now. Still nothing. Was the storm robbing her of her power? Marnie steeled herself for one last try. "*Please help us, Michael. We've got the Book…!*"

Far away in Tantallon, a weak and weary Michael Scot trudged slowly through the castle. "It's your destiny, child. Not mine," he murmured sadly.

In Edinburgh, Marnie let go of her pendant, frustrated by her lack of success. She was also increasingly worried about the weird storm and the intense darkness, which seemed to grow deeper and blacker by the second.

The buzzer rang.

"Marnie, would you get that?" called Dad. "I'm lighting the fire."

A tidal wave of fear rushed through Marnie. She

could think of only one person who would be out in such dreadful conditions – Toledo.

The buzzer sounded again. And again.

"Hurry up, Marnie!" Dad shouted irritably.

Her heart heavy with dread, Marnie approached the door and plucked the security handset from wall. "Hello? Who's there?" she said.

There was a moment of silence before Laura's familiar voice blasted through the handset. "Hey, Marnie – it's Laura! Come on, let me in. It's like a *hurricane* out here!"

Marnie relaxed, her hand reaching towards the door-release button. She was just millimetres away when–

"No, no, no, Marnie, *no!*" screeched Edwin, performing a frantic dance round Marnie's feet. "It's not her – it's the Shapeshifter!"

Marnie froze, uncertainty gripping her once more. *Was* it Toledo? She decided to test the caller. "If you are who you say you are, then prove it!" she said.

"What?" Laura's voice sounded angry now. "Come on, Marnie! I thought we were going to the pictures!"

Doubt crept into Marnie's mind. It certainly *sounded* like Laura.

"*It's the Shapeshifter!*" repeated Edwin.

There was another furious buzz and then: "Oh, forget it, Marnie. You're way too weird for me…"

As Marnie hung up, a cross and frustrated Laura walked away into the darkness.

"Who is it, sweetheart?" called Dad.

"Nothing…" said Marnie. "Just some kids fooling around." She scooped up Edwin and hurried along the darkened hall to the safety of her room.

The buzzer sounded once more.

Dad laid down his tongs beside the gently flickering fire and went through the darkened flat to the front door. He picked up the handset.

"Forth Power, sir," said a man's voice. "Come to fix your electrics."

"That was quick," said Mr McBride. He went to open the door, but stopped when he heard Marnie hurtling towards him.

"No, Dad! Wait!" she shouted. "You can't let him in. You can't!"

Dad frowned. "Marnie, come on. They've just come to fix the electricity. Don't be silly," he said.

But Marnie wasn't being silly. This time she knew with utter certainty that it was Toledo. He wanted the Book and he'd come to get it.

CHAPTER TWENTY-FOUR

INTO THE FLAMES

Marnie's dad pressed the door-release button and spoke into the handset. "Come right up to the top floor."

"Dad!" cried Marnie. Then she fled to her room – one thought banishing all others from her mind. *She had to save the Book.*

Thankfully, it was still sitting on the dresser. Marnie hugged the heavy tome to her, before dashing back into the hall. The flat suddenly seemed so small. Where were the hiding places, the nooks and crannies, the heavy wooden caskets with great padlocks? Or was there a better place to put the Book – a place that not even Toledo would think to look…? Marnie shot into the kitchen, yanked open the freezer and jammed the Book into the largest space she could see. Then she slammed the door shut.

Edwin, Ailsa and Bruno had clambered up onto the

kitchen table, where they huddled round a flickering candle.

"Oh, blimey. Oh, oh, oh, it's hopeless," moaned Edwin, flinging a wing across his brow. "We can't defeat Los Contrarios!"

"We've got to," said Bruno firmly.

Marnie shone her flashlight around the kitchen and caught Wolfgang in its beam. He was standing on top of the freezer. "Didn't you say they were copies of you guys?" she asked him.

"Dark and sightless, but copies nonetheless," replied Wolfgang.

"Then you guys have got to win, right?" said Marnie logically. "I mean, how can a copy be better than the original?"

Wolfgang crouched and then sprang through the air to join the rest of the Shoebox Zoo on the kitchen table. "We must protect the Book and the Chosen One," he roared. "Fight to the death if we have to."

Up the stairs they came. Slowly, steadily, unstoppably. The men wore pristine white overalls and the taller of the two carried a strange, wooden box with four domes set into the lid. He leant close to the box. "This is it my chipmunks," he whispered. "The moment for which you were created…"

Toledo and McTaggart slid on shades and white baseball caps, then rang the bell to flat number eleven.

Lightning flashed and thunder rolled as Mr McBride opened the door. He blinked and shielded his eyes from the glare of Toledo's flashlight.

"Here we are, sir," said Toledo, striding boldly into the flat. "Forth Power at your service. No job too big or too small, in and out like a rat up a drainpipe, you wouldn't know we'd been here at all!"

"So what exactly is the problem?" said Mr McBride.

Toledo smiled mysteriously. "We're here to sort out a small *power* problem."

Marnie peeped nervously into the hall. It was him – just as she'd known it would be.

"And how long will this take?" her dad was saying.

"Oh, that depends on the *resistance* we encounter – *electrical* resistance, you understand," replied Toledo, shining his flashlight right in Marnie's eyes. It was as if he knew exactly where to find her. He started walking towards Marnie, his words filled with hidden meaning. "*Resistance* to the flow of *power* can be very dangerous. But we pride ourselves on making small problems go away before they grow up to become a major pain in the posterior…"

"Well, the fuse box is in there," said Dad, seeming nonplussed by Toledo's strange ramblings. "So if you'd like to take a look at that–"

"Enough of this charade!" said Toledo impatiently, snapping his fingers. Immediately, the lights came on. And Marnie watched in horror as Toledo thrust the palm of his hand towards her father. In slow motion, Mr McBride crumpled into an unconscious heap.

"*Stop!*" cried Marnie. "What have you done? *Dad!*"

Toledo chuckled nastily and walked towards Marnie, while a troubled McTaggart gently patted the back of Mr McBride's hand.

"I am Juan Roberto Montoya de Toledo," he boomed. "Master of the Secret Sect of Assassins, Shifter of Shapes and Scholar of the Necromantic Arts." His voice dropped to a deadly whisper. "And you have something I desire…"

Marnie reached for her pendant and its pulsing energy gave her courage, even though her voice was thin and brittle. It was up to her to stop him. "But I'm the Chosen One," she said logically. "Only *my* hands can touch the Book."

"And only your hands can give me the book," Toledo said. Then he seemed to realise that Marnie wasn't going to back down. He waved his hand imperiously. "Oh, fear not, girl-child. I have my little darlings to help me…"

McTaggart laid the wooden case at his feet and reluctantly flipped open the clasp. The lid lifted to reveal *Los Contrarios* in all their evil glory. Like the dark reflections of a hellish mirror, they looked both like and unlike the Shoebox Zoo. They gurgled unpleasantly, stretching their arms, wings, necks and legs before scuttling across the floor towards Marnie's room.

"Go on, my dainties. After them!" he commanded. "Little black wolf – you stay with me."

★

Edwin, Ailsa and Bruno had run for their lives – through Marnie's room, over the window sill and onto the roof. They were cowering in fear behind the chimney pots when their evil twins found them. And then the great battle began – a battle to the death.

The black snake was first to attack. She selected her opponent, slithering quickly towards Ailsa and rearing into the air, jabbing with her deadly tongue. Twisting wildly, she pounced repeatedly. But Ailsa blocked every single move, hissing back at the deathly snake.

Meanwhile, the black bear was preparing to attack Bruno, who had transformed from a meek, friendly bear into a snarling, wild beast. His teeth bared dangerously, Bruno lunged again and again at the ferocious black bear.

Edwin had truly met his match. He and the black eagle were playing a dangerous game. They battled on the rim, jumping back and forth across the open void of a chimney pot, where one false move would mean certain death…

And throughout, *Los Contrarios* – in vile, unearthly voices – recited the wicked incantation that their master had taught them…

"*When you are dead, your flesh I shall eat,*
Tear out your eyes and cut off your feet,

Twist off your wings and saw through your bones."

The Shoebox Zoo fought bravely, but *Los Contrarios* were fuelled by a terrible power that it seemed Edwin, Ailsa and Bruno could not hope to beat.

But then the black eagle made a mistake. With a terrible shriek, it raised its wings and lunged at Edwin, who summoned up all his courage and leapt across the gaping hole of the chimney pot – and landed, safely, on the other side. The black eagle lost his balance, teetering on the edge before falling down…down… down inside the chimney to the fire that was lit far beneath.

Ailsa's battleground had shifted to the TV aerial. She and the black snake hissed and spat at each other, wrapped round the metal prongs. They had a view – if they'd had time to look – of the entire murky city. *Zap!* A bolt of lightning forked through the sky and struck the black snake, fizzling and burning until nothing was left but a wisp of smoke.

Bruno was still fighting, angrier and fiercer than he'd been in nine hundred years. The black bear was forcing him backwards, closer and closer to the roof's edge – and certain death. Bruno moved backwards. The black bear moved forwards. Backwards. Forwards. Backwards… Then Bruno played his ace. He moved aside as the black bear moved forward – and his opposite plunged over the edge…to certain death.

They were safe.

But Marnie was in terrible danger.

She wrenched open the freezer door to check that the Book was safe. There it lay, squashed between the waffles and the frozen peas. "So what do I do now?" she whispered urgently.

Wolfgang answered from his vantage point on top of the freezer. "Trust in the power that is in you, Marnie."

"Bring me the girl-child!" bellowed Toledo. Nothing happened and nobody replied. "Must I do everything myself?" he roared.

McTaggart, who was busy trying to revive Mr McBride, ignored him.

Toledo angrily stamped around the flat, using his powerful magic to fling open doors and cupboards. Only one door remained stubbornly shut – the door that led through to the kitchen and living room. He reached for the doorknob, then screamed in pain as it sizzled beneath his touch. Not to be beaten, Toledo lifted his palms upwards and concentrated.

The door started to shake, then the floor... Soon the actual walls were rattling violently. But the door remained closed.

Behind the living-room door, Marnie clenched her fists and concentrated like never before. Her pendant burned and throbbed, sparkling with pure energy. Wolfgang howled encouragement. But Toledo's evil energy was gaining. Now a wind had whipped up, stirring up the contents of the living room like a mini tornado.

"I can't hold it!" moaned Marnie, instinctively backing away from the door.

Boom! The door — and the last barrier between Marnie and Toledo — exploded into a million pieces. Toledo stepped neatly through the gaping hole and headed towards her. The black wolf followed on his heels.

"Where is the Book, girl-child?" Toledo hissed. "Don't be coy. You know I can make you tell me."

"You can't…" whispered Marnie. "You won't."

"Where is the Book?" repeated Toledo with menacing slowness.

Wolfgang leapt down from the freezer. "I'll tell you," he said. "If you promise to make me human again."

Toledo laughed in triumph. "Finally, someone has come to their senses," he said, picking up the tongs from the fireplace.

For just a second, Marnie believed Wolfgang. And then, she knew that he was trying to trick Toledo.

Unfortunately, so did Toledo. He snapped the tongs closed, holding Wolfgang in a vice-like grip. Sparks flew, but the Shapeshifter didn't release the tiny wolf, who whimpered in pain.

"Did you really think I'd been played for a fool by the misbegotten son of a foolish wizard?" Toledo hissed. In a flash, he whisked Wolfgang over to the fireplace and dangled him over the leaping flames.

"You wouldn't!" cried Marnie desperately.

"I'm afraid he would, lassie," said a forlorn McTaggart.

"I'll count to ten – or perhaps eleven," said Toledo, his voice deadly calm and utterly determined. "Give me the Book or little Wolfie becomes firewood. One… two…three…four…"

Wolfgang writhed in terror above the fiery heat. "Forget about me!" he screamed. "*Don't* give him the Book!"

Marnie watched helplessly. Should she save Wolfgang or save the Book? What should she *do*?

"Five…six…seven…eight," growled Toledo. "I mean it, Marnie!"

And Marnie could see that he did mean it. So, with leaden feet, she crept to the freezer and pulled open the door. Then she dragged out the fabled book – *The Book of Forbidden Knowledge*. Toledo's eyes widened in ecstasy and followed Marnie as she carried the Book towards him.

But instead of handing Toledo his prize, Marnie swiftly held it over the fire instead. "Let Wolfgang go or the Book goes in the flames!" she threatened.

"No, Marnie – you mustn't!" pleaded Wolfgang.

The Shoebox Zoo – who had hurried from the scene of their victory – watched in disbelief.

In an ancient castle on the coast, Michael Scot spoke in a voice that was weak and rasping. "No, child… You don't realise what you are doing!"

"One…two…three…" Marnie was in charge now.

And she knew that if anyone had earned the right to own the Book, it wasn't Toledo.

"Noooo…" cried the Shapeshifter. "You know not what you do…"

"Four…five…six. At least it'll stop two miserable old wizards from fighting over it," she snapped, moving the Book even closer to the flames. And she meant it. She would do anything to save Wolfgang – even this.

"Fool!" spat Toledo. "You will destroy us all!"

"Get out of here," said Marnie, through gritted teeth.

At last, Toledo backed away, his face contorted with hatred. "I will – for now," he said. He looked across at Edwin, Ailsa and Bruno, who watched him from a safe distance. "Where are my pups…my dainties?" he asked, his voice suddenly anxious.

From their proud expressions, Marnie could tell that *Los Contrarios* were long gone.

Fury burned in Toledo's eyes. "I will be back," he snarled. "Even if this traitor will not!"

Before Marnie realised what was happening, he streaked back to the fire and threw Wolfgang into the flames. "Noooo!" she screamed.

Wolfgang howled in agony, his tiny body writhing and twisting in his fiery grave. "Marnie…I'm sorry I failed yoooooooou," he moaned. "Goodbye…" As his voice faded, Wolfgang's blue and gold coat became charred and turned to ash, before the flames engulfed him for ever. For a moment, the face of a proud young

man – his eyes closed as if he were sleeping – appeared among the flames. Then that too was gone.

Without its earthly counterpart, the black wolf – the very last of the evil replicas – could not survive. It exploded into nothingness, wiping Toledo's triumphant smile from his face. He vanished.

Outside, the deadly shadows receded and the daylight returned.

"Well, at least the power's back on," said Marnie's dad, walking past the living-room door that was now as good as new. "Must have dozed off," he mumbled sleepily. "Everything OK?"

All Marnie could do was nod. She gently touched the three shoebox creatures that lay frozen on the rug before her and gazed into the flames. Everything was not OK. It would never be OK again.

And in the Inner Sanctum of Tantallon Castle, a father began to mourn his son.

CHAPTER TWENTY-FIVE

The Day
Of Reckoning

It was morning. But it would take a lot more than daylight to brighten up Marnie McBride. Her eyes roamed around her room, taking in one, two, three… creatures, the Book that had caused so much trouble and Michael Scot. She blinked. *What?* There, in her mirror, was the great wizard. Dressed in a tattered old robe made of sackcloth, this was a much older, much sadder wizard than she'd ever seen before.

"Vanity and pride killed my son," he murmured. "*My* vanity, *my* pride."

It was as if a dam had burst in Marnie's soul. All the pent-up anger came flooding out. "Magic books? Special powers? It all adds up to zero!" she cried.

Michael Scot continued his wretched monologue as if she hadn't spoken. "Wolfgang's death is my punishment. I killed him, as sure as if it were my hand that put him into the flames. For Toledo's hands are

217

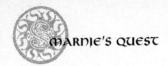

my hands, and ever has it been so…" His image began to fade and his pleading eyes met Marnie's. "I must go now and prepare for the Day of Reckoning. The Book has been opened and without it I'm lost. You must give it to me freely before the sun sets on this day or not at all."

"Wait, Michael. Wait!" called Marnie, but in vain. In the mirror, there was now just a reflection of Marnie's room. "What did he mean when he said that his hand was Toledo's hand?" She looked to the Shoebox Zoo for the answers.

Edwin shuffled his feet uncomfortably. "Oh, a mystery," he said nonchalantly. "An enigma."

"Stop lying!" exploded Marnie. "Just tell me the *truth!*"

Without warning, she was catapulted into a terrifying vision in which a jumble of images chased through her mind.

The Book of Forbidden Knowledge…*a strange, metallic Celtic rune…Toledo clad in a white cape…Michael standing on the battlements at Tantallon…a hand copying the Celtic rune into the Book.*

"*Michael made him,*" murmured the voices of the Shoebox Zoo. "*He fashioned Toledo out of the four elements — earth, air, fire and water… That's the Forbidden Knowledge in the Book — the secret of life itself.*"

Michael stared at a huge, veined, glowing sphere, watching as hands tore a hole in the membrane. A revolting, slime-covered creature clawed its way out. It was Toledo.

The great wizard introduced himself. "My name is Michael Scot – alchemist, astronomer, translator of the ancients, creator of life…your life."

With a jolt, Marnie snapped back to the present to find the Shoebox Zoo staring at her fearfully. "You stupid, greedy, no-good, no-brains!" she yelled. "You stole the Book and nearly gave it to a Frankenstein's monster, who was created by a power-crazy wizard, who thinks that I am the Chosen One and that the fate of the world lies in my hands and now you want me to give it *back* to him?"

The Shoebox Zoo flinched guiltily and Marnie knew without a doubt that it was the truth.

It might be the Day of Reckoning, but the weather was shocking. Rain poured in torrents from an angry sky and in the few steps between her front door and the car, Marnie was soaked.

"Come on, Marnie!" said Dad. "You can't afford to be late again. You've been in enough trouble this term and if–"

"Dad!" Marnie interrupted before he could really get going. "I know that I've been a pain, OK? And that things have been difficult…but I love you."

Marnie's dad looked as if he couldn't decide whether to laugh with relief or burst into tears. "I love you too, sweetheart," he said, hugging her.

Marnie hugged him back. For all she knew, it might be for the last time.

★

In the penthouse suite of the Balmoral Hotel, high above the rooftops of Edinburgh, McTaggart draped the embroidered white cloak round Toledo's shoulders. Underneath, the Shapeshifter was dressed to impress in an elegant tunic and pointed boots – white from head to toe.

"The Day of Reckoning, McTaggart," he said, admiring himself in the mirror. "A day on which you will finally have your freedom – one way or the other." He chuckled at his servant's increasingly worried expression. "Do you think I am blind, McTaggart?" he asked. "Do you really think your treachery has gone unnoticed?"

McTaggart reached for the scimitar that would complete Toledo's outfit. "Treachery, your Magnificence?" His voice trembled.

In the blink of an eye, Toledo was by his side. "The Eternal Wanderer, searching helplessly across the centuries," he hissed. "Self-styled Keeper of the Books... Self-styled fool!" Toledo whisked the scimitar from McTaggart's sweaty grip. "A fool sent to spy on me by his *true* master, without the wit to see that *I* was the one who was spying!"

"Spying, your Excellency?" said McTaggart innocently. "I – I – I don't understand."

In reply, Toledo closed his eyes and raised his palms towards the ceiling. When he lifted his lids, his eyes were filled with pure evil. *Crash!* McTaggart ran as the mirror shattered into eleven hundred pieces.

"Go, slave!" thundered Toledo. "Tell your *true* master that his Day of Reckoning has arrived!"

Marnie reached the classroom just in time to hear her name being called. Ms McKay frowned crossly, but made no comment.

"Laura, I'm sorry about yesterday," Marnie whispered urgently as soon as she sat down. "I can explain—"

"Oh yeah!" snapped Laura. "So what fantasy are you having today, Marnie?"

But Ms McKay wasn't in the mood for class discussions. "It's bad enough you being late, Marnie McBride, without you disrupting everybody!" she said frostily.

McTaggart patted Michael Scot's shoulder gently. "I'm truly sorry, Master," he said. "For all his faults, he was your son."

"I didn't treat him like one, and now it's too late." Michael shook off his servant's hand crossly. "None of this would have happened if you hadn't meddled in things you didn't understand."

Meek and mild McTaggart swelled with anger. "I took the Book so it wouldn't corrupt you the way it corrupted your students, or fall into the hands of that evil monster that your precious knowledge created!" he said bitterly. "And what thanks did I get? Tortured in your dungeons for eleven years and doomed to walk the earth until this blasted Book is found!"

221

Michael blinked at the ferocity of McTaggart's rage. "You know I'm powerless," he murmured. "She has to choose."

"You could *ask* her," McTaggart said quickly. "You could *plead* with her. And if it comes to it, you could *beg*…"

In Ms McKay's classroom, things were going from bad to worse. Marnie was trying desperately to concentrate, but Toledo – invisible to everyone but her – had other ideas. "Dearest Marnie," he simpered. "Give me the Book and this will all be over."

Instinctively, Marnie felt for her pendant, only to discover that her neck was bare… Horrified, she lashed out at Toledo, her flailing arms thwacking Laura by mistake – and tipping her backpack from the desk.

"What are you playing at?" yelled Laura.

Ms McKay loomed above the desk. "Right, Marnie," she said. "Take your backpack and put it in the locker where it belongs."

As Mr McBride pulled up at a set of traffic lights, he spotted something bright and shiny out of the corner of his eye. There, on the passenger seat, was Marnie's precious pendant. Wordlessly, he picked up the silver feather and cradled it in his palm. And when the lights changed, he headed back the way he'd come.

When he arrived at Marchmont School, it was

still pouring. Mr McBride parked, grabbed his outsize golfing umbrella and headed towards the front gates.

As she trudged towards her locker, another voice whispered in Marnie's ear. "Forgive me," it said. "Please, I beg you. Bring me the Book. With it, there is some hope – without it, there is *nothing*."

It was Michael Scot.

Marnie looked desperately all around. The corridor was bare – where *was* he? Then the school bell signalled the end of lessons. "Great," she said, flinging down her backpack.

"Oww!" cried a tiny, but unmistakeably pompous voice.

Marnie quickly unzipped her backpack to find the Shoebox Zoo squished together beside the Book. "Sorry, you guys," she said. "It's just that I've got to get to the castle and I don't know how."

"You're something else, you know that, Marnie?" It was Laura. From her stunned expression, Marnie could tell that she'd overheard every word that Marnie had said to her bulging backpack. "First you were going to share some big secret with me. And then, yesterday, you act like you don't even know me. What is the *matter* with you?"

Feeling like a cornered animal, Marnie faced Laura and said with total honesty, "If I told you, you'd never believe me."

"But I can't help you if you won't tell me what's going on!" said Laura.

So Marnie did – at last. "The Shoebox Zoo, they're alive, only they're not animals, right? They're human beings – students of this great wizard guy named Michael Scot. He lived nine hundred years ago but he's still alive today. And I have his Book of magic, but I have to get it back to him at Tantallon Castle, and the problem is that I've lost my feather." Marnie paused at the end of her epic ramble, too nervous to check Laura's reaction. "I guess I can't blame you for thinking I'm weird, right?"

But Laura was too busy staring at the tiny silver and gold snake who had slithered out of Marnie's backpack. "Are you going to ssstand here chatting all day?" Ailsa hissed impatiently.

Bruno and Edwin hopped out to join Ailsa.

"You must give back the Book!" said Edwin.

"So, do you get it now?" asked Marnie, relieved beyond belief to have shared her secret at last.

Laura was doing an excellent impression of a waxwork dummy.

"If I hadn't gone to that stupid junk shop on my eleventh birthday then none of this would have happened," continued Marnie. "My eleventh birthday," she repeated thoughtfully. How could she have forgotten something so important? She looked at her locker, even though she already knew which number was printed on the door. "Number eleven."

Marnie moved to her locker, opened it and gasped at what she saw inside. She'd done it! "Sorry, Laura," she said quickly. "I've got to get to the castle."

"You mean we're going to be *human* again?" squawked Edwin, performing a victory dance.

"Yes, come on!" said Marnie impatiently, quickly popping the three creatures into her backpack. Then, to Laura's utter astonishment, she clambered into locker number eleven.

CHAPTER TWENTY-SIX

INSIDE THE BOOK OF KNOWLEDGE

"Laura, thank goodness!" called Mr McBride. He rushed along the corridor, water dripping from his furled umbrella. "Have you seen Marnie? I've got to give her this…" On his palm lay the pendant necklace.

"Er…um…yeah," replied Laura, in a dreamlike voice. "She…she's…er…in there." And she pointed to Marnie's open locker.

Mr McBride looked nonplussed. He walked uncertainly towards the locker that was surely far too small for an eleven-year-old girl to hide inside and peered in. Inside, there was no Marnie, but there was no locker either. Instead, it was an opening into a dark, mysterious passage.

Taking a deep breath, Mr McBride poked his umbrella through the locker entrance and climbed after it. Wordlessly, Laura followed.

★

Marnie ran as if her life depended on it, the heavy backpack thumping painfully against her shoulder. The tunnel was dark and forbidding, the floor slippery with mould. Would this lead her to the Inner Sanctum? She had no way of knowing.

Then, behind her, Marnie heard a shrill scream. Fear clenched her heart and she spun round to face Toledo, his white robes glowing in the darkness of the tunnel.

"I have a surprise for you," said the Shapeshifter, smiling malevolently. "You'll never guess who I bumped into." He snapped his fingers and two silent and still figures appeared beside him – their mouths open and their eyes wide with shock. It was Dad and Laura. Toledo had frozen them – mid-step and mid-scream – as they ran to save her. "Give me the Book," Toledo hissed.

"No!" shouted Marnie. "Get away from me!"

Toledo smiled. "As you wish, Chosen One," he said lightly. He snapped his fingers once more and Dad and Laura disappeared from sight. Then he vanished too.

"*No!*" Marnie cried despairingly. She hadn't meant this to happen! Her dad and Laura whisked away to… to…where?! Would she ever see them again?

Now she really *was* alone. She threw down her backpack and slid to the floor, clutching her head in her hands in utter despair.

The Shoebox Zoo struggled out of the backpack and looked anxiously at the Chosen One.

"What's the matter, Marnie?" asked Bruno softly.

Marnie raised her head and stared at the tiny creatures in front of her. "What is the matter?" she repeated incredulously. It would take all the time in the world to explain what was the matter. Instead, she blurted out a reply that she knew would hurt them as much as she was hurting inside. "I am sick of you guys and I'm sick of this entire *Quest*. I wish I'd *never* opened your scuzzy shoebox. Just go away and leave me *alone*."

Edwin and Bruno hung their heads, but Ailsa slithered over the cold, damp ground and onto Marnie's knee. She watched sympathetically as a solitary tear rolled down Marnie's cheek.

"Ssself-confidence and trussst, that'sss what thisss quessst is about – sssomething I have a little trouble with myssself," she confided. "And from one lasssie to another, I think you've been magnificcccent! I trussst you to give usss life and to deliver the Book."

"I'm scared," whispered Marnie. "I don't think I can…" And what was the point anyway? Toledo had taken everyone that mattered to her, hadn't he?

Or had he…?

A twinkling of light blossomed and grew until it filled the entire tunnel. And at its centre, a hooded figure appeared. She looked up and smiled lovingly.

"Mom?" breathed Marnie, hardly able to believe that

she'd appeared just when Marnie needed her most.

"Don't be afraid, my baby," Marnie's mother whispered. "For this is the Day of Reckoning and their fate was sealed long, long ago. Take the page that was written for you. The rest is emptiness, soon to be filled with darkness and destruction." She smiled encouragingly.

A woman's hand placed a final handwritten page onto a teetering pile of pages.

"Trust me," continued her mother. "The Book will find its own destiny. But this last danger the Chosen One must face alone."

The vision faded, but Marnie still felt the warmth of her mother's love. If her mom thought she could do it, then it *must* be true. She suddenly felt stronger and more able to deal with what lay ahead. And in her mind, a plan began to form…

Bruno and Edwin bounded excitedly out of the darkness. "Marnie, look what we found, just lying there!" cried Edwin. In Bruno's paw was the silver feather from her pendant.

"Thanks, Edwin," said Marnie. "But I won't be needing it now. It's yours – wear it with pride."

Bruno performed the honours, sticking the feather into the gap on Edwin's tail.

"This is as far as you guys need to go," said Marnie gently. "I'm sorry if I've been a little tough on you. I've got to do this on my own…"

★

"It's getting darker," murmured McTaggart, brushing imaginary dust from Michael Scot's finest robes. "He's here already."

It was true. The firelight grew weaker by the second. The shadows were increasing, reaching further into the Inner Sanctum. There, the great wizard and his servant awaited their destiny.

"Bring me my staff," said Michael bitterly. "Who knows, by the end of day, you might have your freedom…"

McTaggart obeyed. And, as soon as the magic staff touched his hand, Michael began to pulse with life and new energy. He strode towards the door, his robes billowing behind him, his staff held high. McTaggart followed in his mighty wake.

Toledo appeared from nowhere, blocking their path. "Home sweet home," he sneered. "Fear not, old man. I come not for battle, but to trade with the girl-child – *your wretched life in exchange for the Book!*"

Michael's staff began to sparkle with light. "Earth! Air! Fire! Water!" boomed the great wizard. "From the four elements you were created and, on the Day of Reckoning, to them you shall return!" He pointed the glowing staff at Toledo, who took it from him effortlessly. Michael Scot's great show of power had been just that – a show. Now he was powerless.

"The Day of Reckoning is yours, not mine," Toledo snarled. "Your power is dying, but it is reborn in me – the sole creation of your Forbidden Knowledge!"

He pointed the staff at Michael's head, holding him captive within the dazzling beam of light pouring from it. Michael's knees buckled and he fell to the ground, unable to resist his evil creation's growing power until–

"Is *this* what you two old fools have been looking for all these years?" Marnie walked slowly down the stone steps. In her hands she held the Book. "Doesn't need the hands of a great and powerful wizard to touch it now, does it?" she said. "I'm just a kid, but even in my hands, this Book could destroy both of you." She placed the Book on a wooden workbench. She felt stronger and braver than she had since her mother had died. She could do this – she knew she could.

Toledo lowered the staff and Michael staggered to his feet, both staring greedily at the Book.

"I know your secret, Shapeshifter," said Marnie grimly. "I know who made you. The secret of life itself – that's the Forbidden Knowledge in the Book, isn't it, Michael?" She flipped open the Book and tore the first page from it, before slamming it shut. "I'm taking only what's mine," she explained. "The rest is for you, Toledo."

Marnie closed her eyes and used the power that lay within her, concentrating every last fibre of her being into *The Book of Forbidden Knowledge*. The great tome began to spin round and round until it was just a blur. Then it shot across the workbench, smashing

everything in its path, before flying – *whumph!* – into Toledo's waiting arms.

"You see," said the Shapeshifter to Michael Scot, whose old, weary face was expressionless. "Your precious Chosen One has chosen *me!*" He smiled victoriously and opened the Book. The beautifully drawn words and pictures began to glimmer and then fade from the page. Toledo turned to the next page – blank. And the next and the next and the next. All blank. He slammed the Book shut. "This is *not* the Book!" he said furiously.

Marnie watched calmly. "It's a fake, just like you," she said. "Blank pages just waiting to be filled with all the poison inside you."

The Book began glowing and quivering in Toledo's desperate hands. It grew brighter and hotter, burning him with a searing heat. But he could not let go. Toledo screamed in agony, his body shaking violently as he was slammed against the wall of the Inner Sanctum. Finally, spectacularly, the Book and its new owner exploded in a ball of flame, rocketing up the well shaft to the outside world and whizzing high into the air, hanging motionless for a second and then plunging down into the angry sea.

Marnie and the great wizard walked out into the courtyard. The dark rain clouds had gone – in their place was a glorious sunset.

"Do you think he's gone for good?" asked Marnie

hopefully. She *so* wanted to believe that Toledo was history and that everything was going to go back to normal.

"I don't think there was ever any good in him," replied Michael. "I should have destroyed him a long time ago."

McTaggart appeared at Michael's elbow. "So the Book remains lost," he said. "What about me? When do I get my freedom?"

"Without the Book, I am powerless," said Michael, his voice flat. McTaggart's shoulders sagged despondently. He walked away.

The great wizard turned to Marnie. "You have to find the Book," he said. "The Quest continues."

Marnie stared at him, totally numb. Deep down, she'd known this would happen. Now it was real.

"Er, pardon me," said a familiar voice. Marnie looked down to see the Shoebox Zoo perched on the arm of a wooden bench. Edwin puffed out his chest and held his wings wide. "In my capacity as official spokesperson for the Shoebox Zoo, may I offer you our—"

Bruno butted in impatiently. "We knew you could do it, Marnie!"

"We knew you were the Chosen One," added Ailsa proudly.

"Yes, we did," said Edwin, speaking plainly for once.

Marnie managed an awkward smile. "There's something you guys should know," she said. "The Book

was a fake – a decoy created to protect the real one."

"If that's a copy," said Bruno, "where's the real Book?"

Marnie looked at the crumpled page in her hand – the one page that remained of the fake book. Suddenly, the Celtic runes upon it began to rearrange themselves, moving and changing until they formed what Marnie, with amazement, recognised as a Native American design. Then...

A slender, hooded figure rolled a barrel along a clifftop and pushed it over the edge. The wooden barrel tumbled down, down, down towards the ocean below, disappearing under the waves with an almighty splash before bobbing above the surface. Slowly, it drifted out to sea.

Marnie rubbed her eyes to clear the vision. "It's across the great ocean," she said to Michael. "It's at home."

Michael Scot grasped her shoulders and spoke earnestly to Marnie. "Then you have to find it, for it is your destiny." He let his hands drop and walked back to where McTaggart waited for him.

"But what about Dad and Laura?" Marnie asked anxiously, turning to see Michael and McTaggart vanish into thin air.

"Don't worry, Marnie," echoed the wizard's voice. "They're safe. *Trust me.*"

Marnie stood on the edge of the cliff, staring out over the churning water. Questions flung themselves round her mind like the waves that crashed against the rocks far below. If *The Book of Forbidden Knowledge* was across the great ocean, how did it get there? Who took it – and why? And how could she follow?

Just as she'd hoped that her Quest was over, Marnie McBride knew that it had only just begun.

the QUEST CONTINUES

*But when the clock does chime again, and hours
and minutes pass,
The cogs will turn relentlessly behind the cloudy glass,
Until the Dawn Queen's faithless hand shall
open up the Book,
Then death and darkness will descend on all
who dare to look.*

When Marnie's father sends her back to Colorado to stay with her grandparents for a holiday, it seems that destiny is taking a hand in her search for *The Book of Forbidden Knowledge*. But she soon learns of a second prophecy, and that an evil Chosen One seeks the Book as well…

Look out for the next Shoebox Zoo novel, coming in March 2006 from BBC Children's Books.